SILHOUETTES

Hope you enjoy it!
Dina Bozzoki

Ashley
Williams

Jessica
Shash

SILHOUETTES

The Writing on the Wall

Dina Bozsoki
& the Wilson Central Scribes

iUniverse, Inc.
New York Lincoln Shanghai

Silhouettes
The Writing on the Wall

Copyright © 2006 by Dina Bozsoki and the Wilson Central Scribes

iUniverse books may be ordered through booksellers or by contacting:

iUniverse
2021 Pine Lake Road, Suite 100
Lincoln, NE 68512
www.iuniverse.com
1-800-Authors (1-800-288-4677)

Cover design by Matt Sharer.
Back Cover Images: Cedarvine Manor—Dina Bozsoki's Creative Writing Class, Leon Denny who was the inspiration for the book, and Mr. Larry Kernagis, principal of WCHS.

ISBN-13: 978-0-595-39269-8 (pbk)
ISBN-13: 978-0-595-83665-9 (ebk)
ISBN-10: 0-595-39269-5 (pbk)
ISBN-10: 0-595-83665-8 (ebk)

Printed in the United States of America

Acknowledgments

This novel would not have been possible without the help of so many. We'd like to thank Leon Denny for the inspiration to use Cedarvine Manor in Lebanon, Tennessee, (about 30 miles east of Nashville, Tennessee in Wilson County) as a setting for the book and Landon, the Concierge/Curator at Cedarvine Manor for graciously allowing the creative writing class to come and explore the house and grounds (and for all the disposable cameras, too!). If you'd like to see the real place, go to **www.cedarvinemanor.com**. The backing and support of the Wilson Central High School (Lebanon, Tennessee) faculty and staff, especially the overwhelming encouragement of principal Larry Kernagis, helped bring this project to fruition. A special thanks go to readers Jodi Davis, Nancy Pullen, Glenda Davis, and Cindy Kernagis for their time, talent, and extra eyes to catch those details which didn't add up, and of course, finding those stray spelling or punctuation errors. To the WCHS Photoshop guru, Matt Sharer, we give accolades for the beautiful cover.

A very special thanks goes to Dr. Charles R. (Bob) Kaelin, M.D., who underwrote the cost of getting this project off the ground and published. Ten percent of our sales will go to the ARK Foundation (named after his children Ashley, Robbie, and Kristin) to provide student scholarships.

I would like to thank my husband, Mike, for listening and not complaining through this entire process when I spent my spare time with the novel instead of spending that time with him. I would also like to thank Mike Whicker at F.J. Reitz High School in Evansville, Indiana, for inspiring me to tackle this and showing me a class could get it done. The most important thanks of all go to the students who took on this project and made it all possible, the Central Scribes. The Scribes include Amanda Cecil, Bridget Creighton, Benjamin Greaves, Angie Roach, Jessica Shook, Jessica Smallwood, Sasha Stamper, Blake

Thorn, Casey Todd, Trent Weekes, Teresa Wille, and Ashley Williams. Two of the Scribes, Jessica Shook and Blake Thorn, deserve special thanks for their 1860s period dressing to promote the book at local events, and a heartfelt thanks goes to those who came in after school to work on the finishing touches long after the class was over. We hope you enjoy it.

Prologue

❁

Cedarvine Manor Convalescent Home, October 12, 1864

She entered his office with innocent tears in her brilliant blue eyes that contrasted so much with the pinned-up flames that rested upon her head. She was so young, but her face resembled that of a person who had seen far too much and was weary from it all. How was it that someone so childlike could have experienced so much?

"He…he died during the night…in his sleep," Adeline choked out through sobs that wracked her lithe body.

"Oh, Addie. I'm so sorry. You did recognize that this could be a possibility, didn't you?" asked her loving cousin, Dr. Phillip Newborne Jennings, sitting behind the massive oak desk.

Adeline had come to the manor a year prior to meeting the soldier who had eventually melted her iced-over heart. Before the war, she had been the belle of the ball. Every eligible gentleman in the county was lined up at her door, but she had eyes for the one man who had no interest in her whatsoever. He was a tall man of about 32 who told her that he liked her but wanted someone older, not a child. Oh, how she had pleaded and cried until she had no more tears in her eyes to shed. She had tried explaining that age had nothing to do with it, but he refused to listen. Roger had simply apologized and closed the door on her and their relationship.

Unfortunately, that was not the end of her heartache. She was to be a blushing bride to William VanDerMeer, a soldier she nursed to health in Murfreesboro, but he never showed to their wedding. He left her standing at the altar, her beautiful face streaked with the anguish of that betrayal. Will had run off with some Jezebel on that very day, and that was when she decided to close her heart to love.

Now here she stood with another scar to bear from the loss of a love. Oh, the pain of loss was enough, but this man had become Adeline's world, her sun, and her very life. The man had become everything to her, even after she had vowed never to fall for another man again, to die as the spinster that she thought herself to be.

When she left Phillip's office, she knew exactly what had to be done. Marching down the long solemn passageway to the room that meant so much to so many people—to the wall that was a memorial to those who missed their loved ones, to those who needed cheering up, to those who would never see home again—Adeline held her chin high with all of the pretend confidence that she could possibly muster. She walked to the wall, and with the nubby pencil used by many before her, she began to immortalize her pain upon the slate of grainy pine. Only by the grace of God did she manage to inscribe her full message in the rough surface before her knees buckled beneath her. Between waves of self-pity and tears streaming down her face, she heard the soft creak of the door as someone entered the room.

"S-s-s-h-h…it's all right. Let me help you to your bed. You've been through enough for a lifetime, but you still have a job to do," cooed Rebecca in her ear. The sound was gentle, yet commanding. The older woman always knew how to comfort Adeline when things got rough.

Rebecca lifted the poor girl to her feet. She had always thought of her as a younger sister or even at times, like now, as a daughter. The two women limped down the hall toward the room that they shared. When Rebecca helped Addie onto her bed, she asked if there was anything that she could do to lessen the pain.

"No," replied the broken-looking doll. "Wait. On second thought, could you hand me my diary and shut the curtain so that I may write?"

"Of course. Anything you need," whispered the older nurse. After handing her the leather-bound book, she slipped off of the bed to close the delicate white curtain.

"Wait, Rebecca! I forgot to thank you for helping him these last few days. You don't realize how much we appreciated the generosity," she said with a distant smile, her thoughts wandering back to the weeks and months before.

"You are so very welcome. Now get some rest…you will need it," she softly chided. With these last few words she left, closing the curtain that surrounded the young lady's bed.

❧   ❧   ❧

October 12, 1864
Today, when I arose there was a pain so fierce in my chest that I could not breathe. I had awoken with a jolt from a terrible dream. Unfortunately the nightmare did not end.
I cannot believe that he is dead…

CHAPTER 1

Nashville, March 2003

"You want me to do what??" Maddy asked in stupefaction. "A nurse? I can't stand the sight of blood, and you know it!! My nursing career ended during my sophomore year, and you know that, too! I'm an engineer, and you want me to play at being a nurse to some old, sick gentleman?"

"Oh, come on, Maddy, you're such a chameleon. One minute you act the cold and haughty ice princess and the next a screaming woman scorned…"

The blood drained from her face at those last words hurled at her. He didn't need to remind her of their broken engagement. Why she had ever gone against her credo to never have an office romance—and with her boss at that—Ron Lynley, head engineer for highway development at the Tennessee Roadway Engineering Company. Madeline's father, Jennings Hightower, owned the firm, and he had been so happy when she had put her foolish, rebellious dreams behind her of becoming a nurse and followed the route *he* had always planned for her. Jennings felt a kinship with Ron's driving ambitions, so much like his own driving ambitions, and he felt Ron deserved to take over the company upon his retirement. His familial pride wanted his daughter to also have the position. Knowing a woman would never be taken seriously, he had encouraged Ron and given him his blessing to court his daughter. Jennings knew nothing of Ron's dark side—his insatiable need to be in control, his peccadilloes, his scheming ways. Jennings had watched Ron slice away at his daughter's rigidly-held control, and he knew from experience, his daughter's exterior announced "stay back" to any man who might show an interest in her. Ron had swept her off her feet, wined and dined her, romanced her into saying yes to his marriage proposal, and even up to four weeks before the wedding, Madeline never sensed what was about to happen. She had taken a personal day to finish up some final preparations, and as she left the couture bridal shop after her last fitting, she saw them. She started to wave, thinking Ron had had a business lunch in the Tropics Restaurant in the Renaissance Hotel as he often did. But this beautiful blonde, instead of shaking hands at the conclusion of a successful business lunch, turned into Ron's arms and gave him a most unbusinesslike kiss. Worse, Maddy saw Ron return the kiss with just as much ardor.

Her hand dropped to her side, and as she fought back the tears, she knew Ron had hurt her more than any of the others—the high school sweetheart unwillingly torn from her by Jennings, her overbearing father, the college professor who claimed to love her body and soul, until she discovered he was married, and now Ron. She really thought this time when she cautiously opened her heart that she had found the happiness that had been lacking in her life. She ran to her car, and after driving aimlessly for several hours, she found her way home. Still stunned, she staggered into her room, and much like when she was a child, she curled into a small, pitiful mound of pain. She slept, dreamlessly, and when she awoke, she clearly knew what she had to do.

The next day, after several pages went unanswered, Ron called her house to see why she hadn't returned his calls. She calmly told him the wedding was off and hung up. Twenty minutes later, Ron was at her door, and the years of unending heartbreak and pain erupted into a stoic, but deadly calm—much worse for Ron than if she had screamed out what her breaking heart urged her to do.

"Ron, I saw you yesterday with a blonde woman coming out of the restaurant across the street from the bridal salon where I was having the final fitting of my wedding dress."

"Well, so what?" Ron bluffed. "You certainly can't be calling off our wedding because I had lunch with one of our most important clients?"

"Obviously more important than me." She saw Ron begin to retort when she added, "Wait...before you say anything else, can you explain why *that* important client, *that* blonde...*that* one you soundly kissed...*that* one who soundly kissed you back...what possible reason could there be to end a "business" lunch *that* way?"

"What on earth are you talking about, Maddy? I have no idea what you're talking about or who you think you saw, but you're..."

"Ron, how dare you think you can sweep this away as a figment of my imagination. I know what and whom I saw, and I know that was no ordinary lunch. How many other times has this happened? Looking back on all the business meetings lately, it all makes sense to me now why you felt YOU had to be the one to see them successfully through to completion. I guess a deal with a gorgeous woman can be successfully sealed with a kiss." Her words left her drained and Ron seemingly unfazed.

"You're totally overreacting, Maddy! These "things" sometimes happen. When you come to your senses, you'll see I'm right, Maddy. Don't be so archaic. It didn't mean anything anyway, and when you get to work tomorrow, I've got an assignment for you that will take your mind off this silly drama. Your father has given us the most promising and potentially the most lucrative work for the firm. A month from now, if you complete this job successfully, we'll be starting not only the biggest project of our careers, but we'll be starting a new life."

That was all last night, yet here she sat…fuming at his seeming indifference to her pain and outraged at his suggestion to play nurse to some old man. As always, though, when Maddy hurt, she hid the pain, stood taller, and turned the other cheek. Ron sat smugly, knowing he had won again. Maddy was so malleable, and he knew before it was all over, he'd get back into her good graces. Jennings would help him, too. As he watched the play of emotions cross Madeline's face, he laughed inwardly at her naiveté.

"OK, Maddy, are the theatrics over? I knew after a good night's sleep you'd see how you'd overreacted. You know I love you with all my heart, but I'm a man, and sometimes these things happen. It didn't mean a thing, and sometimes we have to do things we don't really like to do to get the business to come our way."

"Oh, really, Ron? I guess if you saw me coming out of a swanky restaurant on the arm of a handsome man, and in broad daylight, embrace and kiss him, you wouldn't have a problem with that?"

"Don't be so obtuse, Maddy. I've explained myself, and I really don't want to fight with you. I always try to do what's best for your father and the company. Jennings understands these things."

Maddy arched her eyebrows, knowing full well that her father would certainly agree with Ron. Her entire life had been directed by Jennings, and even more so after the death of her mother in 1989 when Maddy was fourteen. Because her father worked all the time, and her mother's health had always been an issue, Maddy had learned to not only nurse her mother as best she could, but she had become insulated in the house. She had very few friends because of the hours that she spent by her mother's side. The only real friend Maddy had, Linda Bowers, came from a huge family, and she, too, had responsibilities that kept her busy. At school, they sat next to each other in art class, and in that flexible setting they shared inconsequential tidbits of their lives because they never really had the time out of school to share the consequential happenings of most fourteen year olds. Maddy especially loved hearing about Linda's family reunions. Linda hated them, she said because she was a built-in baby-sitter; Maddy loved hearing about them because as an only child, and with no family close by, she yearned for the camaraderie she saw with Linda and all her siblings. On days when her mother felt like talking, she would ask her about her own family and why they didn't get together and have reunions, but her mother would just say that relatives on both sides of their family were either dead or not worth knowing. When she pressed her mother for more information, Jennings would intervene and scold Madeline for upsetting her mother. She stopped asking after awhile, and when her mother died, her father forbade her to speak of it ever again. Like most young people, she eventually let it go.

At 18, her growing feelings for the quiet, honorable, and handsome Mike Bowers, Linda's older brother, brought her into that loving family environment she had so desired at fourteen. What started out as mild flirtation when Mike would pick up Linda and Maddy from a music rehearsal, or when Maddy would see him working out in the middle of a field baling hay and take him something to drink, grew into a strong and abiding love over time. Having missed the closeness of a simple family dinner, of popped popcorn in the fireplace while watching a movie in the family room with Mike's two younger sisters and two younger brothers, or trudging through the snow to pick out and cut down the perfect Christmas tree, Maddy fell under the loving spell of the Bowers. The huge family embraced Maddy, and she spent many an afternoon and weekend surrounded by the warmth and love of the Bowers' family. Jennings missed the signs of his daughter's budding infatuation, as Maddy spent very little time at home and talked very little to her very distant father. Work and making the almighty dollar consumed him, so it wasn't until that Valentine's Day in 1992 that Maddy came home beaming over the ring given to her by Mike that Jennings noticed his little girl was a young woman in love. In love with a boy from a farm, a farm…the very idea disgusted Jennings. To him, any family who loved the earth more than money obviously didn't have the fiber to give his daughter the things he wanted her to have.

"Daddy, look what Mike gave me! He's asked me to marry him, and we've decided when I graduate this spring, we'll marry. Mike only has one more year to go before he gets his agriscience degree, and I'll work to get that degree in nursing. His parents will let us live in the old smokehouse on their property, and we'll fix it up…and, Daddy, what's wrong?"

"You'll do no such thing, young lady! Your mother would turn over in her grave at the very thought of you marrying that—that farmer!"

"Daddy, you don't even know him or his family. How can you be so judgmental? I love them, and they love me. Mike loves me, and I love him, and you can't stop that."

"Watch how you speak to me, Madeline Elizabeth Hightower. I'll brook no nonsense on this issue. Mike Bowers can't and won't ever give you the kind of life you were born to live. How can you even think to live on a dusty old farm surrounded by pigsties and filth? Your mother raised you better than that, and you won't dishonor her memory by this foolishness."

Maddy looked on in anguish as her father pulled the ring off her finger and settled it into the pocket of his vest. He walked to the phone, dialed a number, and her insides ran cold when she heard her father say, "Mrs. DuBois, does the offer still stand to send Madeline to your finishing school?" He nodded a few times and continued, "Certainly, she can be there by Thursday. Her mother so wanted her to have this opportunity, and since her death…yes, well, I should have followed up on her last wishes. Madeline has no idea with what an amazing opportunity she has been gifted…of course, she'll have the proper attire. We'll take care of it tomorrow when we reach New York. Yes, it *should* be quite a little adventure for her, indeed, and as a Hightower, *she'll do her best.*"

Maddy looked on in horror as she heard her father's end of the conversation. A finishing school? Her mother's last wish? Tomorrow? New York City? Before Mike's name even swam into her mind, she sank to the floor in disbelief in a dead faint.

Maddy started when she heard Ron's voice say, "Earth to Madeline…Earth to Madeline. I swear you looked like you were going to faint. Believe me, Maddy, Jennings has come up with the opportunity of a lifetime for us. Just give me another chance. You won't be sorry."

"Really, Ron? Do you really think I can so casually accept how callously you've broken a trust I thought we shared?"

"Maddy, trust me again. I'm telling you, what you saw was a business ploy and nothing more. It gave us a huge contract over on the east side of town, but what your father is offering us will make that innocent kiss pale in comparison to the money we can make off the Cedarvine proposal."

"Cedarvine proposal? What are you talking about?" Maddy asked.

"Just the biggest road construction project this area has ever seen. It will join the major areas in Middle Tennessee with a crossroads of profits…from transportation to light and heavy industry, to all the peripheral companies that will spring up around it. Our firm has a stake in all of it, and once we own the land, there's an endless possibility of wealth for us, Maddy. For us! Your father and his company will become bigger than any other engineering firm around."

"I don't care about money, Ron, and you know that. That's beside the point, though. What you haven't explained is why I have to pretend to be a nurse? What does that have to do with any of this?"

"Madeline, you know how I use my people skills to get things done around here. Why the very thing you've mistakenly viewed as a reason for halting our wedding was nothing more than a superb acting job. And it got the job done!"

"But…" Madeline interjected.

"No buts, Madeline. In business, we have to do what we have to do. Your father and I are depending on you to help with what could be the biggest coup of our business lives. The reason we need your *expertise* as a nurse is to get us in the door at Cedarvine Manor. The old coot, Leo Dunn, owns all the land we need for this project, and he's in failing health. His children can't afford to hire someone to help him, and they certainly can't afford to put him in a home. His two older children live about two hours east of Nashville, and not only is it a long trip for them to make, but they just can't feasibly be there to take care of Mr. Dunn when he needs them. The property has been in his family for years, but the manor has become a cash cow for him and his kids. They want to get rid of it AND have enough money to put their father in an assisted-living complex. They can't do that unless they sell the property, but Leo won't sell. He's got two or three children…well, they're hardly children. They're more like in their late 30s and 40s, and I understand a couple of them are really getting desperate for him to sell. One son, John, I think, isn't around much, and Leo's two other children seem to act like they wish he'd stay away. He must side with his father on not selling the place, but that's not a problem right now. He's out of the country. We've told his children we'll do our best to help them. Other companies are bidding on the property, but we've got the upper hand because we have what Leo really needs."

Maddy interrupted, "I'm still not quite following you, Ron. What exactly…"

"Pay attention, Madeline. What Leo needs is a nurse, and you've done that most of your life."

"Caring for my mother and barely getting through a year and a half of nursing classes hardly qualifies me as a nurse!"

"It won't take much, Madeline. Pour on that sweet, gentle charm of yours, and you'll have that old man eating out of your hand in no time. If anyone can convince him to sell, it's you."

"That just doesn't seem like a very ethical thing to do, Ron," Maddy countered, "and you know how often I disagree with you and my father's business tactics. Isn't there any other way to win this contract without resorting to deceit?"

"Ah, my dear, sweet gullible girl. Don't look at it as deceit. Look at it as helping your fellow man. Not only will you be giving Leo some tender loving care, but you'll be helping his family out of a difficult financial situation, you'll be providing jobs to hundreds, maybe even thousands of people, all the surrounding counties will gain in innumerable ways, and best of all, we'll start our married life out on an incredible high of success."

"I still don't like it, Ron, and I haven't changed my mind about calling off the wedding. I need to talk to my father about this."

"No, you don't. It was his call, Madeline. You won't get anywhere with him. He wants me…I mean us, to succeed. Think of it as a wedding present from the old man. Now, be a good girl and go get packed. The sooner we get you there, the sooner you can finish those wedding preparations. It's what your father wants. It's what I want. You know it's what you want, too. You're just tired, and that's why you so badly overreacted to a completely innocent business meeting."

Just then, her father entered the office, and winking at Ron, he smiled broadly as his daughter turned around. In his hand, he had a rolled set of blueprints. "I take it Ron has filled you in on our plan to control Cedarvine. Just think of the prestige that will be brought to this firm. I can't begin to tell you, Madeline, how very important this war we wage is to us all. All those competing companies won't even know they've been to battle once we've won the war over Cedarvine."

"Father, I still…"

Jennings took her arm and led her to the door. "Now, Madeline, run along like a good girl. I'm sure you have plenty of things to *prepare for this little adventure, and as a Hightower, I know you'll do your best.*"

Madeline closed her eyes and clenched her fists as the door to Ron's office closed behind her, but this time at hearing her father repeat those words, she didn't faint.

CHAPTER 2

New York City, 1992–93

Mrs. DuBois ran a tight ship in her quaint house in Manhattan, but she still felt sorry for the proud Madeline Hightower. Teaching her the ways of society seemed a losing proposition, as the youthful Madeline acted more like a spinster than a debutante. She also refused to lose the serene southern drawl of her home state, and Mrs. DuBois knew that Madeline would be a laughingstock of the season if she couldn't cure her of it. Of course, there didn't seem to be a cure for whatever was ailing the tightly strung, moody young girl. Her father, Jennings Hightower, had whisked her quickly into the city, and just as quickly whisked himself back out. He'd paid Mrs. DuBois an extra stipend to keep Madeline sheltered from the "horrible" experience (as Jennings cryptically referred to Madeline's dropping in on Mrs. DuBois's doorstep) by keeping the phone and mail delivery unavailable to Madeline. Madeline's mother had been the one to contact Mrs. DuBois all those years ago, believing her daughter deserved more than the local refined, southern-bred education. When she became ill, she couldn't force herself to let her daughter go, but she had told Jennings that should the opportunity present itself after she was gone to send Madeline for a year of "polishing" so she could take her place easily in Nashville society. Jennings found Mike Bowers to be that opportunity. Despite Madeline's pleas to not be sent away, he did the only thing he knew how to do. He took control of the situation and got the mess out of his way. He didn't understand his daughter, nor did he have the time to try. He assuaged his guilt over her tears by telling himself he had made a promise to his wife, and he was doing what was best for his daughter. Over the next several months, he occasionally wrote to Madeline and sent her money and clothes, but he didn't visit or call. Madeline never spoke of him or her home. She just wondered why Mike wouldn't answer any of her letters.

Madeline finished out her senior year at Manhattan's High School for Math, Science, and Engineering, and every day after school she dutifully attended the required sessions on etiquette and comportment with Mrs. DuBois. But she spent the majority of her free time alone in her room or at the piano in the sitting area. At least, thought Mrs. DuBois, she had one of the fine arts mastered.

In the fall, through Jennings' machinations, Madeline found herself enrolled in a small, four-year liberal arts college in New York City and in her very own tidy apartment. He told Madeline that a good friend would show her the ropes of the engineering curriculum, which would allow her to study the field that provided their livelihoods. If that's what it would take to get home, Madeline decided she would do it. Since Maddy had articulated out of most of her general education classes, she found herself drawn to those class descriptions dealing with health care and nursing. Madeline knew Jennings controlled most things, but this was one thing she could keep from him, and for once, she was glad of the distance, both physically and emotionally. She immersed herself in the classes and the labs in the science building, and she volunteered to help at the local nursing home. Her days and nights became a blur of activity, diversions that Maddy welcomed. Time and distance had dimmed the pain of her father's betrayal, and her favorite professor who she also interned for at the local nursing home, Dr. Slade Snyder, brightened her days with his enthusiasm for her work ethic, her outstanding grades, and the pain he saw in her eyes which he inwardly vowed to erase. What began as a crush on her anatomy professor turned into a full-fledged romance when he offered one day to take her for coffee after a strenuous evening volunteering at the geriatric wing of the hospital and covering many code blues.

Flustered as she was, his bedside manner calmed and soothed her awkward fears about expressing her feelings for her teacher, especially when he murmured, "Madeline, don't take this the wrong way, but I feel something for you that I probably shouldn't be feeling. I see pain that I want to heal, and I know I have no business asking a beautiful young woman to even consider thinking of an old man like me in the way I'm thinking of her…and…"

"Please, don't apologize. I'm not that young, and you're not that old, and, well, I'm amazed that you actually feel something for me. I thought you'd just see me as a student, a silly little infatuation. I'm sure lots of students in your class feel the same way I do…I mean, you know…sometimes we fantasize about our professors. Actually, many of the girls in my classes talk about you and compete for your attention. Haven't you noticed? So many of them see you doctors as a way to get out of working for a living. High salaries, nice houses, maids, private schools…"

"Well, many doctors make a very comfortable living, but teaching doctors just aren't in the same league. Is that what you see in me, Madeline?" he laughingly asked as he arched a very handsome brow her way.

"Absolutely not. I don't need a man's money. My family…" She stopped as suddenly as she started.

"Your family, what?" Slade gently asked.

Madeline heaved a great sigh. She hadn't shared any of her pain with another human being since Mike Bowers. She still wondered why he had never answered a single letter, but she reasoned, that was all in the past. It was time to move on. Here sat a man who cared for her, a man who wanted to help heal her pain, and she was ready for someone to share all of her hopes and dreams. She could hardly believe that Dr. Slade Snyder was sitting here with her, admitting his feelings for her, asking her to consider seeing him as something more than her teacher. She was almost 20 years old, and she was ready to take a chance again on opening her heart.

The following months passed as if Madeline was in a dream. She continued to work hard in school and in her internship and volunteer work at the hospital, and on nights when Slade wasn't busy, they cozied up by a fire in her apartment or watched vintage films in Greenwich Village. She had never been happier.

And then one night, her world shattered again. She was hoping to finish up early at the hospital on the chance she might get to spend some time with Slade. Just as she was getting ready to leave, the emergency room exploded with activity. A terrible accident had taken place in the Hudson River Tunnel, and all staff was being called in to help. A passing doctor asked Madeline to help, but she tried to explain that she wasn't a *real nurse* just yet and that she just worked with geriatric patients, helping them exercise or reading to them. Before any of that could come out of her mouth, the doctor shouted, "Now, over there in cubicle six."

As she entered the room, she saw what she was sure had once been a beautiful woman with a ghastly gash from her forehead to her chin. She had never seen so much blood. She whimpered, felt the bile coming to her throat, and turned to leave the room when Slade came bursting in.

"Oh, Slade, I'm so glad you're here. I can't handle this. I never thought that as a nurse I couldn't stomach the sight of blood, but I feel so ill, and I, well, now that you're here…"

Slade rushed by her as though he hadn't seen her. Madeline realized now was not the time to feel fainthearted in this emergency, and she swallowed hard and turned to Slade and said, "I'm so sorry. What a poor example I'm setting as a nurse."

He still ignored her. Madeline chastised herself for her unprofessional reaction until she saw him gently touch the shattered face and then visibly sob out a name. It sounded like *Susan*. She moved to the other side of the bed, and then she noticed the hand that so gently touched this woman's face had a silver wedding ring on it, a ring she had never seen on his hand when they were together. At her questioning glance, Slade made no apology. He turned back to the woman, and as he did, another man scrambled into the cubicle.

"How is she, Slade? Will my sister make it?"

Slade turned to the man who was his brother-in-law, gulped loudly, and became suddenly all business. He yelled for help from the emergency room nurse and immediately began giving orders about this woman's care. He turned only once in Madeline's direction, and then he was gone with the gurney and the woman named Susan. As she stared after his retreating back, nauseated and helpless, the man who had come into the room spoke to her. When he touched her arm, she jumped and fell against a tray of antiseptics and IV's.

"I'm sorry, but you look ill, and, and…you're a nurse. Are you OK?"

"I don't know what came over me. I've never reacted to blood like that before. Actually, I don't think I've ever been in a situation with blood, and it just, it just…" she rambled.

"Miss, do you think my sister will be all right?"

"Well, Dr. Snyder certainly knows what he's doing, and I'm certain…"

The man interrupted Madeline as he said, "Well, of course, Dr. Snyder knows what he's doing, and my sister—his wife—couldn't be in better hands."

"I'm sorry, what did you say?" Madeline swayed on her feet, not believing what she was hearing. It had to be the blood, her light-headedness, the adrenaline of the emergency. *His wife??* She turned and fled the room. The man stared after her retreating back.

Back at her apartment, Madeline huddled in a miserable mass on the floor of her bathroom. Her sobs had long subsided, but the pain remained deep in her chest. "Why can't I find someone to love me? What's wrong with me? Why does everyone hurt me so?" The questions shrieked through her head and her heart, but she knew she couldn't stay there any longer. She didn't feel like she belonged anywhere, but at least in Nashville, she could lose herself. Her father wouldn't bother her, and heaven knew, there was no one else there to pry into her life. Her father had seen to that, too. Madeline gathered the courage to finally call her father and requested a visit home. He told her he was in the middle of intense negotiations with a construction firm to build the road infrastructure around a massive new mall in Tennessee. He didn't encourage the visit, but he didn't discourage it either. She didn't care. She needed to go home. Nursing was out, she knew. Her little rebellion against her father had been an abysmal failure. She didn't care about anything anymore except escaping New York. She placed the call that would lead her back to Nashville.

CHAPTER 3

A forest near Nashville, March 1864

The click reverberated throughout the silent forest, echoing against the shadowy trees that surrounded the small group of soldiers. The man at the head of the column tilted his head, allowing him to hear the forest come alive, putting his loaded pistol back into his belt. Slowly he lowered himself until his ear was level with the grassy earth. Silence reigned triumphant; nothing but the soldiers' rasping breaths disturbed the peaceful quiet. A calm voice behind him said, "Sir…what is it? Do ya' hear somethin'?"

Raising his head up, he glanced at his second-in-command with an intense glare. Clearing his throat, he rose to his full height, standing just below the other man. "Negative."

Disturbed now, the second-in-command inquired, "Then what, Lieutenant, is the reason for your sour expression? Ya' act as if the entire Union army led by Grant himself is marchin' down upon us."

The leader of the group of Confederate soldiers looked sullenly at the other man. He shook his head desolately, turning back to the verdant greenery surrounding him and saying, "Do you hear something?"

Cupping a hand about his left ear, the other man listened intently for a moment before shrugging. "No, sir; nothin'."

"Now that," the Lieutenant said with a glint in his dark eyes, "is the problem." With that he brought his rifle to bear, and shouldering it, looked at the grim determination upon his troop's faces. They were dirt-streaked faces that he had grown to respect, the faces that would never know another peaceful rest without awakening in the middle of a cold night from harsh nightmares, memories of what they had been through.

"I plan to see what in the world brought about such quiet from a forest that is usually so proud to speak to us. Private Larcas, you're in charge until Broodings and I return from our scouting. I want you to send the group of men due northeast until you reach the clearing. Position everyone along the perimeter and allow no one to cross through that terrain. Get a move on. Broodings, come on."

With that the lieutenant gestured toward the man with whom he had been previously conversing. Broodings nodded, the two bearing their weapons before them and striding stealthily through the undergrowth. The two stopped for observation purposes, once more listening for any hint that would explain the empty forest. Eventually, Broodings could take the silence no longer, saying to his comrade, "What in tarnations are we doin' out here, Mordy? We shouldn't be doin' this. We could get ourselves killed! Don't ya' care about your men?"

Lieutenant Jacob Mordecai Lee raised an interested eyebrow, smiling at his companion. "Well, I felt like taking a walk. This ceaseless marching with an entire platoon of soldiers is giving me quite a crick in the neck."

"What?" cried Broodings, "Ya' mean we came out here for nothin'?"

"Well, that was our intended purpose anyway, was it not? To discover the great "nothing" that perturbed this forest. Don't get me wrong, Charlie, I adore the routines we do every single day, marching back and forth through this forest, and then doing it all over again the next day, but…"

Charlie Broodings sighed with dismay. "But what?"

"But it's getting old. When is this war ever going to end? A nation should know something is wrong when it is sending its own soldiers against each other, dividing families, and sometimes even condemning them to death by the hand of a brother from the other side. I can't stand the thought." Mordecai leaned against a tree, setting his rifle beside him.

"So ya' make up false alarms to stretch your legs and break the routine, hmm? Your third cousin would be very ashamed." Charlie leaned against a tree facing his friend, his army uniform crisp and without a solitary wrinkle to be found, an imitation of what the army thought of itself: perfect.

Mordecai chuckled slightly before responding. "What would I ever do without an insubordinate soldier such as you?"

"Well, you'd certainly be much less rebellious all the time, I'm sure," Charlie replied sarcastically, winking at his friend. Suddenly the silence was broken as a gunshot rang out against the governing stillness of the forest. The scant sunlight *bleeding through the gaps in the canopy sent rays of heat careening down upon the two soldiers, both exchanging brief glances as they listened for the source of the noise. After a while Charlie spoke up. "Perhaps it was merely one of the men havin' some fun?"*

Uncertain, but hopeful, Lieutenant Mordecai nodded. "That Talberry fellow always was a strange one. Most likely he wanted to murder an innocent creature prowling about the land." A second gunshot echoed through the forest. The two soldiers immediately grabbed their weapons and ran as fast as their legs could carry them toward the source of the gunfire. After leaping over a log that was in his path, Mordecai hurriedly checked to reassure himself that his rifle was ready to fire as the two neared the clearing.

Holding up a hand, Charlie stopped Mordecai's relentless race toward his goal. "What are you doing, Charlie, sto—"

As his friend's hand clamped down over his mouth, Mordecai saw the reason for the necessity of silence. Multiple Union soldiers were standing several yards away, hiding behind an overturned tree beyond the outskirts of the clearing, firing at the Confederate soldiers who were between the clearing and the line of Union soldiers.

"Mordy, be still…they must've caught everyone unawares, formin' a line of soldiers around our circle of troops…sneaky and devilish, aren't they? What say we dance with the devil this day…"

Charlie brought his weapon up, taking his hand from Mordecai's mouth. The two spread out, nodding in unison as they prepared to fire upon the soldiers directly ahead.

Charlie raised one hand, signaling with four fingers.

He dropped a finger as Mordecai felt his breath catch in his throat.

A second finger dropped as sweat began to build up upon Mordecai's brow and blur his vision.

One finger was remaining when Mordecai pressed the trigger too soon.

A loud explosion issued as the bullet was sent on its way toward its target, burrowing into the back of the closest man and dropping him to his knees in agony. As he fell, Charlie fired a single shot, slaying the man who turned around to see what the problem was. The remaining two men turned around and hurriedly tried to load their weapons.

Suddenly, remembering his pistol, Mordecai hurled his rifle at the two soldiers, sending one man sprawling backwards, dropping the bullet he had been trying to load. The other man did not seem affected, loading the gun and cocking it toward Mordecai, who had just gotten his pistol out, yet had no time to raise it, for Char-

lie had also hurled his rifle, though he was much more accurate. The bayonet attached to the end plunged into the soldier's chest. Mordecai smiled faintly in appreciation at his friend before discharging his loaded pistol at the fourth Union soldier, struggling to rise. He wouldn't rise again.

Charlie rushed over to Mordecai. "Sir, are ya' all right? What are we—"

"Charlie."

This one word silenced Charlie in mid-sentence. His throat seemed to grow dry, emitting no sound but a barely audible rasp. He watched with fascination as Mordecai approached the soldier who had Charlie's own bayonet embedded in his chest. Mordecai crouched low, giving the soldier a stricken glance.

Mordecai frowned down at the soldier, who glanced up at him with wide eyes, a dreaded fear sprouting in his mind that outweighed his loyalty to his nation. The Union soldier put a feeble hand upon the rifle, which Mordecai removed gently, confusing the soldier. Nevertheless, the soldier decided that begging for his fading life was better than bleeding to death. As he started to speak, blood exploded from his mouth, covering his lower lip and chin in crimson. "Mercy, please...anything, stop..."

Mordecai heard Charlie stop directly behind him. "What should we do with this 'un?"

Shaking his head and squeezing his eyes shut, Mordecai pondered. Finally, he reopened his eyes, looking at the soldier, and his face voiced the apology he could not make. He quickly pulled the bayonet from the soldier's chest. "What is your name and rank, soldier?"

The Union soldier sputtered more blood out as he said, "H-help...don't wanna die, sir...I'll do anything..."

Mordecai sighed as Charlie abruptly stepped up to the youthful soldier and said, "Hmm...perhaps you should just answer the questions we inquire, boy."

"Private Karl Simons, sir!" the soldier said with a painful expression written clearly upon his face. Sweat cascaded down his brow, mixing with the fresh blood and sending searing agony to lighter wounds he had received from the deceiving branches of the forest.

"Well, that's a start," Mordecai said to Charlie. "Now, let's move onto more pressing matters. What the hell are you damned Yanks doing here around Nashville?"

The soldier let his head loll back against the ground. His eyes closed momentarily before cracking open once more, appearing a bit dimmer than previously. "This is not a coordinated attack, if that is what you wanted to know." He stopped long enough to cough several times, furthering the staining of his uniform with scarlet dedication to his country. "I was part of the attack force commanded by Brigadier General Sturgis and Colonel McCook that participated in the battles at Fair Garden."

Mordecai interrupted, "Fair Garden? That is quite a ways from here."

"Yes," the soldier agreed, "but it was also a while back. It happened January 27. After our success—"

"Partial success," Mordecai interrupted. "If you have not forgotten, your precious General Sturgis decided to further his victory by attacking General Armstrong's cavalry division...which had been reinforced with three infantry regiments after Sturgis learned of their location. Ended with a nasty retreat, Sturgis running away in a very dignified manner, I might add."

The Union soldier laughed bitterly, spitting in Mordecai's direction. "We all know what happened. You Confederates might have slain more of our soldiers with your devilish trickery, but it was still a victory for my nation."

"Ah, so now you're back to being loyal to your 'nation', are you? What if they found out you were betraying them right now?"

"Yes...I don't..."

"Now...we both understand where you came from, but why are you here now?"

The soldier tried to catch his breath as his chest heaved up and down. "Well, after Fair Garden, there were many regiments of soldiers that were assigned to scout out further territory and possible locations that would be worthy to take by force. This regiment is one such scout force." He began to cough once more, but no sound came forth. He suddenly struggled to breathe as tried to answer them. Mordecai and Charlie exchanged worried glances.

Mordecai spoke softly. "So...you're just a scout force from the main army under General Sturgis? You came here by happenchance? But...you seemed to be coordinated and knowledgeable about my soldiers' whereabouts. It cannot be a mere 'chance' occurrence that you stumbled upon my men and caught us unawares in a trap. I do not believe that fact for one second."

"Well, believe what you will, you...you...rebel..." And with that last gasp, Private Karl Simons departed this world, his eyes staring up at the empty expressions on the faces above him. Two fingertips tentatively came to rest upon either eyelid, gently covering the dark orbs below. Mordecai pulled his hand back and closed his eyes, resting his head upon his knee, at a loss of what to do.

Charlie started. "What are we goin' to do now, Mordy? We don't know what the current situation is; there might be hundreds of Union troops here, or maybe just these four! We can't be sure this youth was telling the complete truth. Half-

truths won't get us anywhere." Charlie held his head in his hands as he sank to the ground and fell against a tree, his face contorted in a pained expression of sorrow and failure.

Lifting his head, Mordecai noticed Charlie mimicking his posture of defeat. Mordecai would not allow Charlie to lose faith now. "Have faith that we shall get through this…and we shall," Mordecai replied solemnly, striding confidently over to the deceased soldiers and retrieving his and Charlie's rifles. With precise strokes he cleansed Charlie's bayonet upon one of the dead soldier's uniforms. "Now, stop your sulking, and let's go. We cannot abandon our friends to heartless fiends such as these."

"You're right…as usual…we need to first find out what the situation is, how many troops we're up against and such," Charlie responded with a quivering voice, grasping the rifle in nervous hands and tucking it under the crook of his arm. He stood and saluted Lieutenant Jacob Mordecai Lee before turning around fully and trudging away, followed by his superior officer, who hurried to catch up.

Shortly after walking past an immense tangle of vines dangling amidst some trees nearby, the duo found one of their own Confederate brethren hiding beyond the web of vegetation. Charlie stopped to sigh, lunging forward and gripping the man by the scruff of his neck, tearing him from his hiding place. Mordecai jumped with alarm, saying, "Christopher Lowell, what in the world might you be doing?"

A voice spoke up from behind them. "He was a distraction…bait…in case any Union soldiers made their way to our position."

Turning around swiftly, Mordecai saw twelve soldiers standing before him, all weapons trained upon him. With a grin Mordecai said, "Mad Max, what are you up to, you old rascal? Playing with the enemy's mind again?"

"As always," the large man who had previously spoken said with a flourish of his arms, dropping the gun to his side.

"So, who have we here?" Charlie said inquisitively, admiring the formation the dozen soldiers had created so fluently.

Mordecai laughed as he said, "I have no clue why they are here, but these are the best of the best. This was my old squad before I was transferred to the current regiment we are both in, Charlie. These are the soldiers who rose above the rest of the troop. They are more suited for…shall I say, more 'personal' errands?"

At this, the men surrounding them snickered lightly, exchanging sneering glances. Mordecai gestured to the leader of the ragtag group of soldiers.

"This old dog is Maxwell Baker, my comrade from past battles. He and I have a long history together. He was always my second-in-command when I was leading these sharpshooters. When I left them, the total number dropped from fourteen to *thirteen, an unlucky number indeed...for the enemy, that is, since Max here was appointed the position afterwards."*

Maxwell sent a smile throughout the group as he chuckled wholeheartedly. "Indeed, old friend, those Union swine never escape the wrath of my rifle," Maxwell said with a wink at Charlie, who appeared to shrink back.

Mordecai gestured to the others. "Yes, yes, we all know, Max. These soldiers are the highly trained sharpshooters that they appear to be...well, maybe not so much in appearance as in actions. Hunting down Union boys is their sole duty, however unlawful it may appear, and in whatever fashion that pleases them. Charlie, the thirteen men standing before you now are the ones who work behind the scenes...you won't read about them in any text you'll ever find. Though, if I may say so, the name is quite catchy at the moment."

Charlie frowned. "Which is?"

"Baker's Dozen," Maxwell said with a snicker. The entire group shook their heads at this incessant joke.

"Well, I find it quite catchy indeed," Mordecai said with a shrug. Turning to the soldiers, he raised a brow. "And what, pray tell, are you folks doing out here?"

"Doing what we were made to do: playing the fox and chasing the rabbit," exclaimed a calm voice from the back of the group. Mordecai smiled warmly at this voice, the voice of an old friend who had been like a brother to him.

"Justin, you're still alive?" A hint of sarcasm tinged Mordecai's tone.

"Lieutenant Lee, I'll always live to haunt your dreams," Justin said with an elaborate bow. "We've been tracking these vile creatures ever since they crossed our path six days back. It seems they were bound and determined to reach this forest."

"Strange behavior for mere scouts," Mordecai replied.

"Yes, very," Maxwell agreed with a nod, clutching his rifle tighter in his hand.

After surveying the group, Mordecai frowned. "Where is everyone? I see that Michael and Ryan are here, but please prove me wrong in thinking they aren't the only others who have made it thus far."

"Well," Maxwell started with a sad face, "The war has been raging on for ages now, finally trickling to a dull roar compared to the stormy waves rushing over us like before. I...I guess without your guidance a few men drowned by these terrible waves. It has taken its toll on our friends, I'm afraid. That's what war seems to do best."

Mordecai let his head lower painfully as he cherished past memories he had experienced with the original thirteen in his crew. With an unshed tear, he dismissed the images. A gunshot rang out loudly nearby. "Max, I think we've found what you've been looking for."

Max raised a brow. "The Union dogs…?"

"No, my friend…the rainbow that comes after the storm. We finally will receive an opportunity long awaited: to avenge our brothers, now mere casualties of a war that is long overdue to end," Mordecai said solemnly, giving the newer faces a warm gaze. "Now, Justin…let us play the fox. Shall we catch the rabbit?"

"We shall," Justin nodded in concordance.

Guns loaded, the group rushed through the underbrush, using thick trees as cover lest any Union bullets spew their way. Mordecai stopped, holding up a hand to halt their progress. He surveyed the surrounding territory before gesturing for Maxwell. He pointed to the right side of the forest and said, "Max, I think we need to split up."

"I agree," Maxwell said with a nod.

Maxwell motioned, urging six of his soldiers to move behind him and to the right, therefore dividing the forces in half; the men all bid brief farewells to each other, then grew silent once more.

Mordecai brought his rifle to his shoulder, saluting his friend. Maxwell returned the gesture, and then they both returned to their former stances. "I'll send Charlie with your group," Mordecai stated. "He's a good friend; he'll be of assistance in a time of need."

"Thank you, Mordy; we'll take good care of him," Maxwell said with a grin.

Charlie seemed annoyed by this notion, but said nothing. He merely saluted Mordecai and then treaded to the other side of the group with a frown upon his face.

With that note, the two friends turned away and strode off, going their separate ways with their soldiers, while Charlie reluctantly headed off with Maxwell and his men.

Mordecai heard several shouts, urging him to run faster. From a short distance away he saw the line of trees that formed the large clearing, an open area that doomed any soldiers lurking near it. All of Mordecai's regiment had been on the edge of it.

He could immediately tell many had escaped with their lives, running to the cover of the forest to harass the Union soldiers assailing them from all directions. Mordecai's fury was engulfed by a sudden concern for the lives of his soldiers. "Fan out, men. Keep the enemy engaged at range. You are sharpshooters, not close range fighters. Keep it that way. May God be with you all."

Taking cover behind the trees, the group began to peek around, hunting for targets. At a sudden movement from his left side, Mordecai urgently whispered, "Port side, fire!"

From all around him bullets rang out against the hot afternoon air, a slight breeze sailing past him and seeming to carry the bullets even quicker. At the discharging of so many rifles, the Union soldiers hiding had all looked up toward Mordecai's direction, meeting the bullets head-on. Not one bullet was wasted.

Justin happened to comment upon this fact, saying to Mordecai, "Interesting, their every folly seems to be their demise."

Mordecai grinned. "Perhaps it would be fairer if we disarmed ourselves."

Suddenly, return fire reigned in the dark forest. Mordecai's smile dropped as a cry rang out near him, and one of the soldiers fell with his hand clutching his chest. An old comrade of Mordecai's from previous campaigns had been hit. Michael Kalson's crimson hands tried to staunch the flow of blood in vain; the kindhearted man's eyes glazed over as he toppled to the cold earth with a simple thud, a very unfit ending for a complex thing such as life.

A second volley rang out as Union soldiers from elsewhere let loose a blaze of death, this time from behind Mordecai's position, nothing shielding them from the onslaught. Two more men dropped. One of the two was Christopher Lowell, the first soldier they had sighted who had been bait for any Union troops. The pain in their eyes before death was agonizing to see, forcing Mordecai to look away. More gunshots rang out as the Union soldiers were attacked without warning by Maxwell's forces, which annihilated every soldier with a vengeance.

Nodding his thanks to Maxwell, Mordecai noticed several men missing from Maxwell's own group. Charlie stood with grim determination beside Maxwell, yet he appeared to be smiling…but it might have just been Mordecai's imagination…or was Charlie pleased with the death ensuing around him? Mordecai made a mental note to speak with him about this apparent blood lust later, but at the moment he was in a predicament that he did not desire to be in.

Loading his rifle with another bullet, he brandished it before him. Turning to look beyond the trunk he hid behind, his eyes widened with dismay as several Union soldiers ran toward his small group of soldiers with their weapons held before them. One of the attackers, a ragged salt and pepper beard covering his face, was wearing a uniform with an insignia similar to Mordecai's, which meant he was the obvious leader of this force.

Images of soldiers and Mordecai's close friends breathing their final, pained breaths drove his poor soul to madness. Letting a frenzy overtake him, Mordecai shouted at the top of his lungs, sending a bloodcurdling scream reverberating throughout the woods, the forest echoing his misery as the soldiers felt a slight chill upon their bare necks, hairs standing upon end in anticipation.

The Union soldiers paused momentarily as Mordecai came charging from his cover, surprised at such a frontal assault. With a simple compression of the trigger, Mordecai let sail a single bullet, sending one of the soldiers to his bloody demise, fate not smiling upon that lost individual. A sudden gleam of light was reflected in his eyes, blinding Mordecai temporarily, causing him to shield his face, though he managed to catch a glimpse of the Union lieutenant bearing his razor-sharp saber down upon him.

Mordecai barely had time to bring his rifle to bear in a horizontal pose, letting the saber ricochet from the weapon, freeing Mordecai to swing his rifle and connect with the chin of another approaching soldier. The crack signaled the breaking of his enemy's jawbone. Suddenly his old ally, Justin Adams, was beside him with a fierce expression, plunging his slender bayonet into the stomach of an approaching soldier and twisting madly, ripping it out through the rib cage of the man in a spray of crimson. The open jaw pouring blood and the haunted expression of death from the young Union soldier's face forced Mordecai to turn away from Justin's carnage.

Without any warning, a saber flashed again from behind them, connecting with Justin, who was unaware of the danger. The thrust of the blade was ill-timed, as it barely scathed his arm. Justin turned around, only to see the hilt of the saber coming toward him. It rendered him unconscious as it connected with the side of his head. As his friend collapsed, Mordecai saw that the other two soldiers from his group, one being an old friend, Ryan Cadderston, were nowhere to be found for aid.

"Where are you, Max? We need your help!" Mordecai's plea went unanswered. He soon realized he had said 'we,' when, in fact, he was all alone, his comrades either unable to help him or already among the lost.

The lieutenants were the last soldiers left standing, the other soldiers either dead or in a state that was not fit for combat. The Union veteran held his blade vertically before him and bowed his head slightly to honor Mordecai's final attempts to bring about victory. The Union soldier prepared to lunge forward and end the fight with a final plunge, leaping forward and letting sail his blade. Mordecai could take this man's insolence and ruthlessness no more. With a swift sidestep Mordecai was out of the path of the blade, whipping his rifle butt up and connecting with the other man's left arm with a crack of bone, forcing his opponent to grasp his weapon in a one-handed grip now as his injured arm hung limply at his side.

Mordecai dropped the gun and slowly unsheathed his own saber. With a sudden feint, Mordecai's adversary was upon him again. Mordecai watched closely *and ignored the false attack, deflecting the true strike that came from the opposite side. As their blades clashed with a ring of steel, Mordecai shoved as hard as he could, slowly pushing the weaker enemy lieutenant backwards.*

Just when Mordecai thought the battle was over, the enemy gave a final thrust and Mordecai felt his own weapon slide from the other blade, the Union lieutenant pushing off and cracking his elbow toward Mordecai and striking the side of his head. Mordecai sensed he might yet perish. As stars shone before Mordecai's eyes, he stumbled to the right, falling upon the earth, his blade flat upon the earth a few feet away. He raised his head as he saw the crazed Union soldier position his blade for an overhead slash that would end the battle rapidly.

"A fine attempt, good sir, but not even close to my superior class," the Union lieutenant said with a sneer. Mordecai closed his eyes as he awaited the final stroke of fate.

A shot rang out against the silence that pervaded the forest. Cautiously Mordecai opened his eyes. He noticed the Union Lieutenant glancing down at his chest, where a deep scarlet stain was beginning to form in a circular pattern, spreading rapidly. Harsh blue eyes dimmed before lids began to droop. The blade fell from frosty hands, the lightly bearded man turning around once before stumbling to the ground in a heap, a bullet hole in the back of his uniform. Standing behind him was Maxwell with a smoking rifle.

"Thank God! I was wondering when you were going to show up!" Mordecai said with a shaky voice, a smile that had once been forming instantly shattering as he saw that his friend was bleeding profusely from a wound to his side, likely from the razor-honed edge of a bayonet blade. "Max!"

"Don't worry about me, Mordy, we have other problems…your friend, Charlie, I'm afraid he's—"

"Dead?" Mordecai finished for Maxwell. "Well, a great many of my friends seem to be that way…it can't be helped now. We have to move on, we have to get out of here!"

"Is everyone…gone…?" Maxwell started to fall forward as he saw the dead bodies littering the forest around them. Catching his friend, Mordecai gently lowered him to the ground. Maxwell struggled to rise from his position upon the cold earth, managing to kneel before Mordecai, one hand clutching his injured side, the other his rifle. "I—"

"Max," Mordecai interrupted, "What happened—"

A shot rang out against the silence of the Union commander's death. Maxwell went even colder as his body reverberated from the impact to his back that had apparently been intended for Mordecai. Hurling himself away from Maxwell with a flourishing roll, Mordecai grabbed his saber, grasping it and hurling the weapon with all his might toward the location where he had seen movement. A cry rang out. A Union soldier tumbled backwards with the saber driven into his back. A voice called out, "Hurled with utmost precision for once, I see!"

Mordecai twisted around to see Charlie smiling at him. With a dazed look Mordecai said, "What are...oh, yes, I guess it was. But, you're dead, aren't you? Maxwell said—"

"Do I look dead?" Charlie replied as he grinned up at Mordecai.

"I guess not, but..." Mordecai, dazed, confused, and grief stricken, looked hollowly at Charlie. His eyes widened as he remembered Maxwell. Turning to look at his friend's body lying upon the ground in a puddle of blood, Mordecai grew sick, doubling over and gagging. He quenched his sadness by replacing it with hatred, which urged him to not give in to his desire to show weakness. Mordecai straightened, the pit of his stomach rumbling with distaste as he tried to forget the sights he had just witnessed.

Charlie waved at him wildly. "Let's go! Who knows who else is still alive...sadly many of your friends aren't, I fear, unless they were hiding. I'm sorry, Mordy, perhaps they escaped..." Charlie gestured and Mordecai shook his head wildly, trying to tear the images of his deceased friends from his mind.

"Hurry, Mordy! I know this nightmare seems unending, but we must *move!"*

With a shake of his head, Mordecai cleared his head. The two struggled through the brambles and bushes that littered the forest, making sure to stray far from the path itself, too open an area to present themselves in. Thorns managed to cut through their uniforms, forming small fissures that represented the brutality of the circumstances. It seemed like eternity, but the two finally caught a sign of movement from a nearby tree. Mordecai gestured to make sure Charlie had sighted it as well. Both men readied their short-range bayonets attached to the end of their rifles, hands slightly shaking from the viciousness of their kills.

With a savage roar Charlie leapt around the tree, brandishing his sharp weapon, though at the last second of recognition he shied his blade away, stumbling and falling to the ground in the process. Mordecai proceeded to stumble over him. When the two were untangled, Mordecai was helped up by the soldier they had been intent on slaughtering. He turned out to be one of their own.

Mordecai sighed as he cursed. "James Hissen, what are you doing outside of your patrol? Where is everyone?"

The frightened individual backed away, leaving Charlie to pick himself up. "W-what others?"

Charlie rolled his eyes. "The soldiers with you, in our group, fool!"

"D-dead! All gone!" Hissen crouched down, dropping his weapon in the process. "No one here but me...someone betrayed us, the Unions were behind our position."

Mordecai gasped with anger as he ground his teeth. "You're telling me this...this carnage was caused by one of our own? I cannot believe we have a traitor in our midst! Was this traitor planning this from the very start?"

Charlie started. "No sir, chances are that that someone had more family on one side than the other, and he felt himself in a position to benefit his true side, to stay loyal to them, even if he had to betray the ones he had grown close to. Likely he saw an opportunity, a chance to redeem himself for choosing the losing side in this war."

"Well," Mordecai said slowly, "It appears that you have a good understanding of this person's motives..." Mordecai slowly dropped his hand to the trigger on his rifle, raising it up fractionally.

It was then that Charlie Broodings fired upon his lieutenant, his commanding officer and former friend, the bullet hitting him from close range in the left side, managing to graze a rib as the bullet tore through him. Flailing his arms wildly, Mordecai fell back with a surprised look in his eye. As he hit the cold earth, he heard a second bullet being fired, Hissen falling beside him with a gunshot wound to the head. As he felt the blood drain from his injury, Mordecai gasped, "Tell me, brother, why?"

Charlie frowned sadly, though his expression seemed false to Mordecai. "Were you not listening just then? I'm sorry, I really am...but I've always had my loyalty directed toward my Union brethren. At least a majority of my family is there, more than I can say about your beloved Confederates. Your ideals and goals are not to be trusted. I was approached two days ago by Lieutenant Almington—the man who was disrespected by being shot in the back by your friend, Maxwell. I found that to be extremely annoying, so I had one of my comrades fire into the small of your friend's back. Quite a shot, I must admit. He saw you grasp your saber and began to run away, but I warned him you were horrid at throwing blades...he was just as surprised as I was when the tip of your saber was suddenly protruding from his gullet."

Mordecai glared at Charlie. "You...? You had Maxwell killed? You orchestrated this...this massacre!"

"Don't feel too bad, my friend," Charlie said with a smile, "You'll go down in history! Yes, I shall be known as the Betrayer, but you shall be known as the valiant hero who died in glorious battle after destroying the entire enemy force with scant aid; isn't this what you always wanted?"

"No, not like this," Mordecai said sadly, letting his head drop to the earth. He stared up at the canopy above him, sunlight streaking down into his eyes and blinding him.

"Well," Charlie began, "It's too late now. What is done is set in stone. There is nothing more to add to this story. I shall write the ending, not you. It ends however I decide."

"But..." Mordecai tried to move, failing to do so in the end. "You killed Union soldiers...why? If you allied yourself with them, would they not get angry at hearing of your disregard for who you murder?"

"I had to cover my tracks...what if the attack failed and the Confederates won? It was necessary. Besides, Mordy, everyone who knows of this is dead now. Or, at least, is about to be." Charlie winked at Mordecai, who did not even see it. He had accepted his fate. Charlie continued to gloat. "Yes, so, you'll be dead and I'll be on the winning side. It works out for us both. We both get peace. Though, that was really a pathetic question to ask; really, Mordy, where would I be if I deserted from the start and didn't wait until the end?"

"You'd be dead!" A gunshot rang out across the forest, forcing Charlie Broodings to grip his side in agony. As the astonished look glazed over on Charlie's facade, Mordecai managed to glance past him to where Private Talberry stood with a smoking rifle, a few other injured Confederates standing off to the side of him. Among them was Ryan Cadderston, who had apparently run off during the fighting to search for help. With a burst of speed the overweight soldier, Talberry, was at Mordecai's side, though a fog appeared to be forming a hazy blanket over his eyes as his body grew numb...

The last thing Mordecai saw was Charlie Broodings plummeting forward to the earth. Mordecai winced as darkness covered his eyes, and he groaned, "Charlie..."

CHAPTER 4

Lebanon, Tennessee, April 2003

"I won't sell my house, and that's final!" Leo Dunn argued with his daughter as he was waiting for his new home-care nurse to arrive. He wasn't exactly antici-pating the arrival; the word dread would be a far more accurate verb. That was the other topic of argument with his children that day.

About five months earlier, Leo, who lived alone, had taken a bad fall down the stairs. He had lain unconscious for three hours until his granddaughter, Alchemy, came by for a visit and called 911 when she found him at the foot of the stairs. It was a frightening event for the whole family. Leo's children, David, 49, Melissa, 45, and John, 35, all agreed that he was getting too old to live by himself. They hired a nurse, without his consent. Leo, however, a stubborn, 86-year old man, refused their wishes and argued relentlessly with his children. To add to the pain of driving him into an early grave, they were trying to make him sell his house, the house he had lived in since he was twelve days old. Leo couldn't understand the need for this. The children, however, were only think-ing about the best interests of their father. David and Melissa didn't live close by, and though John did, he was out of town more than he was in it. He loved the house as his siblings didn't, and he worried endlessly about Leo. They knew he would have to be put into a "home" soon, but they didn't have the money for it. If they sold the house, that would be more than enough money to take care of Leo until his time came. And it just so happened that at the same time they began considering this option, a phone call was made to Leo and all three of his children, making an offer they almost couldn't refuse.

The Tennessee Roadway Engineering Company had recently mapped out a plan to build a new highway that would connect Highway 231, which ran in front of Leo's house, and was the main road in Lebanon, Tennessee, to Highway 70, which ran through the neighboring community of Watertown. This road would eliminate miles for someone who commuted into Lebanon from Watertown on a daily basis; also, it would cut down on the traffic on I-40 around the Lebanon area. The miles of land that would be used for the construction of the highway were dotted with houses and farms. All the owners of the homes that would need to be torn down had been contacted, and all had agreed to sell. Leo, once again the stubborn old man, did not agree.

His phone had been ringing off the hook for months with pleas and bargains, but Leo wouldn't even consider. Then his children began receiving the calls. They were a little reluctant at first, until the TREC offered to send a home health-care worker, free of charge, to stay with Leo until he decided to sell the house. But what if Leo decided not to sell the house? His children weren't optimistic. They were realists, and they knew their father better than anyone else around. The man in charge, Ron Lynley, was an extreme optimist; he assured them that Leo would sell his home to them.

The sound of the doorbell interrupted Leo's thoughts and brought him back to the present.

"She's here," Leo mumbled into the receiving end of the telephone. Melissa was growing tired of her father's childish behavior.

"Please, just make the best of it, Dad," she pleaded with him. "I talked to her over the phone, and she seems to be a very nice young lady. She was polite and showed a very compassionate side."

Leo said his good-byes and hung up the phone, still angry with his children and their impulsive decisions. They hadn't even discussed it with him first, he thought bitterly. He made his way slowly to the door; ever since his fall he had to walk with a cane, and it hurt him to travel long distances.

"I'm coming!" Leo shouted to the unwanted stranger. He decided that even though he absolutely hated the idea of having a live-in nurse, he was going to make the best of a bad situation. He even admitted, if only to himself, that he was losing the capability to care for himself any longer.

Madeline waited patiently outside for her new "client" to welcome her into the house. As she stood there, she had a moment to look over the outside of the house. It was a nineteenth-century, white antebellum mansion. The white siding and the huge stone chimneys complemented each other well. The elongated windows allowed for much sunlight to stream into the interior. In the front of the house was a small balcony accessible from the second floor, directly above the front door. An identical one was located on the left side of the house. All in all, the view from the outside gave the house a very simple appearance, and even though it looked like it needed cleaning and a paint job, it was breathtaking nonetheless.

Just then, the door opened, and on the other side stood an old man with a cane. He was taller than she, about 5' 9", with silver-streaked dark gray hair covering his head. Although he had to use a cane, he had an incredibly straight posture. His craggy face seemed tired but his bright, blue eyes showed no signs of tiredness, just impatience. They gleamed handsomely and were filled with a kindness and insight she would soon come to understand.

"Hello," Madeline broke the silence. "My name is Madeline Hightower, and I'm your new home-care nurse."

"Well, I don't exactly need a nurse, but I'm Leo. Won't you come in?" He stuck his hand out and she responded by grasping it quickly and firmly.

She stepped into the house and closed the door behind her. The first thing she noticed was the beautiful, wooden staircase. It shot up and curved to the right. The floor she stood on was a patterned, hardwood floor; it stretched into the two adjoining rooms. To the left was the sitting room. A dull, creamy yellow paint covered the walls and located on the far wall was an enormous stone fireplace. To the right was a bedroom, which looked spacious and comfortable.

"You have an amazing home, Mr. Dunn," Madeline remarked.

"Thank you." Leo was always happy to hear compliments about his home. "This house has been in my family for eighty-six years. I have been living here since I was only this big." He pulled his hands apart about eighteen inches.

Hearing this saddened Madeline when she remembered the real reason she was here in the first place. But just like the many times before in her life, she would not let her emotions control her. She had a job to do, and it would be done.

"Could you give me a tour of the house?"

"Certainly," Leo answered almost triumphantly; for Leo, showing his house to others was the equivalent of showing off a trophy for someone else. Cedarvine Manor was Leo's pride and joy, even though it looked as if it could use some tender loving care.

"Just lay your bags down on the floor, and we will start with my bedroom," Leo motioned to the room on the right. "Um, since my fall, the kids moved all my things downstairs, so there wouldn't be much of a need for me to go up there anymore." Leo pointed towards the staircase.

Madeline set her things on the floor and made her way toward the bedroom. He opened the door and ushered her in. The walls were a medium blue, not dark enough to be navy, and not light enough to be cyan; however, it was somewhere in the middle, that perfect medium. There was another fireplace, used often it seemed, in the center of the room. A large bed with a quilted comforter was pushed up against the far wall to the left. The only other furniture in the room was a small wooden nightstand next to the bed and a matching chest to the right.

They left his bedroom to continue their tour. They went back into the foyer, where this time, Madeline noticed a little more. There was a golden chandelier hanging from the ceiling, a bit tarnished looking, and a painted scene following the staircase from top to bottom, was one of lush, green trees and low-lying bushes. It all was beautiful, but it seemed to be worn and tired like Leo. It just didn't sparkle. As they started to walk into the sitting room, something caught her eye.

"You have a piano?" she asked Leo. Madeline walked over to the old piano, situated in the alcove underneath the staircase. How long had it been since she played? She couldn't remember. But the notes were still there, engraved into her brain.

"It's been here since my family bought the house, and the people we bought the house from said it had been here since they bought the house. No one knows how to play, but my ma thought it would be a nice addition to the foyer area. So, it's been right there ever since. My kids complain when I spend the money to have it tuned, especially since no one plays it, but it's such a beautiful piece, don't you think? I bet there's been all kinds of songs played on that old beauty. Do you know how to play, ma'am?" Leo questioned Madeline, as she stared longingly at the piano.

"Yes," she replied, "a little bit. But it's been a long time. I haven't played since I lived in New York in 1992, and before that, I don't think I'd played since my mother died. Before she got sick, she used to sit with me for hours on end and teach me every song she knew. Once she died, I guess I just lost interest, and then my father got rid of the piano."

Leo took notice of the sadness in Madeline's voice and also thought that her father must be a very despicable man to get rid of his late wife's possessions that his child loved so dearly.

"Well, maybe, if you ever feel up to it, you could play something for me. I would love to hear it played at least once before I'm gone," Leo added with a grin. Madeline realized she had let her guard down. She quickly regained her composure, and they continued to the sitting room. In spite of its disrepair, the creamy yellow of the sitting room made it an ideal room to gather and socialize. Crackling fires in the fireplace during the winter would be the perfect complement to an already cozy room. Madeline wondered what it was about this house that made it so inviting.

Behind the sitting room, there was a dining room. Above the dark, pockmarked mahogany table hung another chandelier. This, too, seemed to glisten dully as the afternoon light hit it. The door that stood between the sitting room and the dining room was a side entrance with a terrace above it. Coming out of the dining room, there was a hall that went behind the stairs. Looking left, it led to the huge country kitchen full of windows to let maximum sunlight inside, but again, the sun seemed to have a hard time penetrating the grime of years of neglect. The kitchen had at least twenty or so large and small chestnut cabinets lining the walls, and straight out the door one could either go to the foyer or to the right side of the house where there was another large, arched door leading outside. Instead of going outside, they followed the hall to the stairway that led to the second floor. Leo turned to Madeline at the foot of the staircase.

"Do you mind helping me?" A red flushed face exposed Leo's embarrassment at being unable to help himself. Madeline simply smiled and interlocked her right arm in the crook of Leo's left arm, placed her left hand on his forearm, and helped him up the stairs. When they reached the top of the stairs, there was small sitting room to the right. A big door in the center led out onto a terrace. Windows on either side of the door allowed for ample amounts of sunlight to come into the room. The room, although painted a cheery, green color and full of overstuffed furniture, was dusty and had a musty smell, yet it seemed comfortable and inviting. The rest of the upstairs appeared to be full of bedrooms, but the doors were closed.

"This is Alchemy's bedroom," Leo introduced her to the first bedroom upstairs. "She is my granddaughter, but she stays here often, especially with her dad, John, being on the road so much. He feels so much better having her here. Alchemy's a free spirit and a pretty darn independent young lady. She thinks because she's a senior in high school that she should be able to stay by herself at her own house. I love her dearly, and she keeps me young. She takes good care of her old gramps, and she loves this house, just like me."

"How old is she?" Madeline questioned Leo.

"She just turned seventeen," Leo smiled as he talked about his beloved granddaughter, and Madeline could sense the two shared a special relationship, but then she saw a sadness frost over his bright blue eyes. "Alchemy was only four years old when she lost her mother to a drunk driver."

Madeline murmured polite condolences, and as she stuck her head into the teenager's bedroom, the first thing that caught her eye was the dark purple color on the walls. The next thing that caught her eye was the number of posters hanging on the walls. There were different bands and movies, but they all seemed...dark. Her bed had black sheets and orange pillows. Madeline wondered if Alchemy's mother's death had affected her more than anyone realized, but to lighten the moment, she said, "Well, this is an interesting...I mean, different...decor," and stopped herself from commenting further.

"Yes, our Alchemy is very unique and definitely her own person, which is more than I can say for the rest of our family," Leo remarked. Leo scowled as he thought of his daughter Melissa and her older brother David. They'd moved out as soon as they started college. They had never come back, except to visit on holidays and make the obligatory stop on a birthday or Father's Day. They had their own lives, and Leo didn't begrudge them that. They just didn't feel at all about Cedarvine as he did. He shook away his melancholy thoughts and turned back to Madeline.

"Sorry, my old mind just wandered off there for a moment. Ready to move on?"

They moved on to the next bedroom. Thus far the only two rooms in the house that had nicer furniture and were newly painted were Leo's room and Alchemy's room. It seemed that all the other rooms upstairs had old, battered furniture. The first one they looked at was to the left of Alchemy's room. It was dark because all the curtains were closed. The musty smell made Madeline sneeze.

"You allergic to something?" Leo asked, knowing quite well that the dust brought on her sneeze. In this room, the bed was smaller; it didn't have a fancy comforter, just plain white sheets. There was also a stone fireplace in the center of the room, just like the one downstairs. In the corner of the room stood a wooden chest for clothes; on top of the chest was a single hairbrush. Madeline walked over to examine the hairbrush. It was silver and obviously an antique, with little designs all over the handle and the back of it. Every room they went into after that was either very similar or exactly the same, but each room had different little knick-knacks lying about. One room had a beautifully decorated jewelry box; Madeline was curious as to the contents of the box, but she knew she had no right to pry. Another room had a very beautiful porcelain doll with curly, red hair and bright green eyes. The last room in this part of the house was not a bedroom but an office. It looked like it hadn't been used in a long time. The musty smell and the dust on the furniture confirmed Madeline's assumptions.

"You won't have a need to come into here ever," Leo told her. "It's just the office of one of the former owners. A doctor. I use the old desk for my papers, and I used the room more when I slept on the second floor. But if I need insurance papers or whatever and am too tired to try, one of the kids will get them for me when they visit. Or Alchemy. She loves rummaging through all this old junk." Leo smiled at Madeline as he closed the door.

"Let's head back this way, and I'll show you which one will be your bedroom." Leo turned expecting Madeline to follow him. But she stood there for a minute.

"What's behind that door?" Madeline pointed to the room next to the office.

"That one?" Leo asked, already knowing which one she was talking about. "Oh, that's just a spare room. There's nothing in there." Leo began to hobble away, and this time Madeline followed him.

He stopped halfway down a second hallway. "This is going to be your room," he said. Leo turned the doorknob and pushed the door open. It creaked slightly; there was no light whatsoever in the room. Leo stepped in first, leaving Madeline outside. He pushed open the curtains, and the sunlight flooded in, like a dam opening its gates. The bed in this room was small, just like the others. There was a small wooden side table, a matching chest to the left, and a bookcase full of books in between the windows. On the floor was a stack of blankets next to the bed. A collection of pictures, four in all, were on top of the chest.

She let her curiosity overcome her this time and made her way to the chest. The sepia prints graced the old golden frames. She noticed on the bottom right corner of all four pictures, there was a name engraved in black, bold letters. Slanted upwards, she read the name Brady. It must have been the man who took these pictures, thought Madeline. The first one she picked up had a picture of a man in a white coat, similar to modern lab coats. He was seated at a desk, not even paying attention to the person taking the picture. He seemed to be concentrating very deeply on his work. The picture looked as if it were from the 1800s. The picture directly to the right of that had two younger men in it. They were in a hospital room. One young man was lying in a bed, his arm bandaged, but he was smiling for the camera. The other man was on crutches at the foot of the bed. He, too, was smiling. They seemed to be pretty happy for being in a hospital. The next picture was one of the house. It was taken from the front yard, and it also appeared to be from a long time ago. The house looked a little different back then. It looked new, and the railings for the terrace were wooden, instead of wrought iron. There was a horse and carriage waiting in front of the door, but there were no people in the picture.

The last picture really struck Madeline as peculiar. She was completely lost in it. It was a simple picture. The setting was a porch with a swinging chair in the corner and a door to the left of it. There were two young people sitting on the porch swing, a man and a woman. They weren't paying attention to the camera. The man was smiling at the woman as the woman was glancing at a book in her lap. She looked happy. She wore a white uniform, and she had on a nurse's cap over the curls piled high on her head. The girl's face looked like one from a dream and seemed so familiar to Madeline. Just then, Madeline glanced into the mirror hanging directly in front of her on the wall. She realized now where she had seen that face before. The girl in the picture looked just like her.

CHAPTER 5

Cedarvine Manor, Lebanon, Tennessee, April 15, 1864

'Jacob Mordecai Lee…such a strong name for one who looks so innocent and youthful.' As Adeline worked to change the bandage on the wound in his torso, thoughts like this began running through her head. She didn't know why she was thinking so much about a man who she hadn't even seen awake, for he had been unconscious since he had been brought in three days ago. Especially considering Adeline's luck with men. Roger Wells, her first true love, closed the door in her face when she pronounced her undying love. Adeline's second mistake, William VanDerMeer, broke her heart and honor when he jilted her at the altar. She vowed not to let this man get to her, no matter what. She couldn't handle another heartbreak. She decided she was getting way ahead of herself on this one. She had to get her imagination under control. This war had been too long and life disrupted, which was why she decided that she had become so fanciful.

As Adeline finished up, her hands moving mechanically, she felt him stir beneath her hands. She rose up with a start. Her first thought was to get her cousin, Phillip, the doctor, but he had left this man in Adeline's care, and she wasn't going to shirk her duties. She went over to him and pushed his disheveled, brown hair out of his face. "Come on, Mr. Lee. You can do it. Open your eyes," she willed him to wake up. "Please, you have to wake up. You are my responsibility, and I will not have you lying there forever." His eyes began to flutter open, and he looked around in confusion.

"That's it. Welcome back." Adeline smiled down at his face.

All of a sudden, he had a look on his face like he was petrified. "Get…get away from me you…you, Yankee!"

Adeline looked at him absolutely stunned. "Mr.… Mr. Lee, please, calm down! You are in an infirmary. You must sit still and not get excited!" Her words were of no avail. He just sat up straight in bed yelling for his gun. Then something registered in his face, and he fell back on the bed clutching his side.

"There, see know? That's what I was trying to tell you. Just lie still, and I'll find you something for the pain." She rushed over to the cabinet and searched for a bottle of laudanum. They were out. Adeline grabbed the emergency bottle of whiskey they had on the back shelf and blew the dust off the top of the bottle. "Mr. Easting doesn't come with the supplies until Saturday, so this will have to do." He took a big gulp and visibly relaxed. He kept his eyes open like he was afraid he'd slip back into emptiness once again. He reached out and took her hand.

"Charlie…No…Union…MAX!!!!!" He still wasn't making much sense.

"Take another sip. It will help you to sort through your muddled thoughts. It's all right. I'll take care of you." He did as asked. Adeline realized he was still holding her hand.

"Promise?" he asked.

"Yes," was all she could reply.

Adeline thought he must have been puzzled or embarrassed by his outburst for when he opened his eyes and looked at her, a slow, uneasy smile began to creep up in the corner of his mouth. "It's all right, ma'am. I think I'm done with the lunatic act for the moment. The next show is this afternoon. Do come and have another glimpse of a man deranged."

Adeline looked in the mirror above his dresser and realized that her countenance had a worried expression. She had always had a problem with her emotions showing on her face. She smiled at him and replied, "Mr. Lee, how can you manage to joke in a situation such as this?"

"Do call me Mordy…it takes my mind off the pain," he answered with an 'aw shucks' grin that showed off the dimple on his cheek.

Adeline sucked in a mouth full of air and counted to five before she could speak again. "Well, now that you're awake and competent enough to make light of your situation, I'll leave you to your own devices so I can check on the other patients. I also need to let Dr. Jennings know that you've awakened. He'll be ever-so relieved to know his doctoring helped and that you've come back from that black space."

Adeline was turning to go when she realized he was still holding her hand. She looked at him questioningly and saw an imploring look in his eyes. "Miss, can you sit a moment so that I can tell you something? Please?" he added when he saw her reluctance to comply. Adeline sat down on the chair beside his bed that she had occupied many an hour before while he had been unconscious, watching over him. When he was sure that she was settled and ready to listen he began, "Thank you, thank you," he repeated, "for watching over me. I thought it was a dream, but now that I have heard your voice, I know it was you. I remember your voice coming to me in all the confusion. You were always soothing and gentle. It helped that you would read to me or just sit and talk. I think I recognized some of the things you read to me, and being able to think about something other than the pain made it easier to will myself out of this dark space."

It was obvious that he was finished making his lengthy speech. Adeline could see that it cost him a great deal of strength. She could also see that he was not used to saying 'thank you' or else she would have tossed his gratitude aside and acted like it was duty rather than pleasure that drove her to it. Instead, she replied almost shyly, "I just wanted to do something, and I didn't know what else I could do."

"It was enough." That was all he said before his eyes flickered shut, and once again he was sleeping soundly like he hadn't been out for three days straight. Adeline knew he would wake up out of this one, so she pulled the blankets up under his chin. She looked around the room that she had occupied, sometimes even all night, for three days so that she could be there when he awakened. The rooms in the infirmary didn't look like regular hospital rooms. Dr. Jennings had furnished them with several of the bedroom suits that his father, Rial, had purchased for the mansion. They were very comfortable and not like army cots; it gave off the ambiance of a home, not a hospital. Adeline walked out of his room and went to check on the other patients. None of them had begun to stir. They probably wouldn't until Rebecca, a nurse and a friend, came on duty with her. Adeline checked the time; it was half past six, and Rebecca started at seven. She started toward the kitchen to begin breakfast. On the way, she stopped by Lieutenant Lee's door to see if he was awake. He was still resting, so Adeline continued on to the back of the house where the kitchen was located.

In the kitchen, she made up some oatmeal and toast. Food supplies were low, and this was the best they could offer at the moment. By the time she had finished heating the oatmeal, Rebecca walked in.

"Sorry I'm late, dear. It's just a splendid day today, and I had to go out this morning for a little stroll on the grounds. You look in high color this morning. Anything new?" She looked at Adeline suspiciously and cocked an eyebrow. Adeline looked at her honest weather-beaten face, work-hardened hands, and gray hair. She had come to be the closest friend she had ever had.

"Becca, Lieutenant Lee woke up this morning at six o'clock. I was there and…"

Becca interrupted, "Slow down, dear! Catch your breath and tell me what happened." She led Adeline to a chair in the dining room, and Adeline told her what had occurred that morning.

"Like I said, Lieutenant Lee woke up this morning at six o'clock. He was confused at first, and then all of a sudden, he thought he was still at war! He called me a Yankee and started looking for his gun! Can you imagine? I got him to calm down, and he became quite coherent. He was in so much pain, so I gave him some of the emergency whiskey."

She paused and then told Becca about his ending speech. "He said he could comprehend some of what was going on around him. He thanked me for staying by his side and reading to him and keeping him company. He said I kept his wits from leaving him completely."

Adeline looked at Becca to see what effect this announcement had on her, for she was the only confidante Adeline had in this house. Rebecca knew about Adeline's abject history with men, and Rebecca had quite an interesting one herself, so she had said to Adeline. Rebecca looked thoughtful and then said, as if to toss the subject aside, "Did you write that down in the report? I'm sure Dr. Jennings would be interested. You know what a strong interest he has in the workings of the mind?"

"I looked for him after I left Lieutenant Lee, but his study door was shut, and you know when his door is shut, we dare not disturb him. I'll tell him everything during rounds. But, Becca, what do you think about what he said about me?"

"We'll talk later, Addie. Breakfast is getting cold."

Adeline helped her gather the trays together and brought them to their weary patients, wondering all the while why Becca wanted to change the topic. Adeline said her good mornings to the other patients, but her mind was elsewhere. She wanted to go check on Lieutenant Lee, but she still had to go about her daily routine with the other patients. It was about noon before she could get away to see him again. He hadn't been awake for his breakfast, so it was sitting on a tray beside his bed. When Adeline walked in, she was shocked to see him sitting, although doubled over, on the side of the bed.

"Lieutenant…! Mordecai…! Lee…! I don't think it is a good idea for you to be attempting this so soon. Let the doctor see you first. Let him decide when it is best for you to attempt to move. You must rest. Let me make sure you haven't pulled any of the sutures out of your wound."

Adeline moved beside him, all business, and helped him lie back down. His ashen face, labored breathing, and closed eyes told her he had attempted too much, but oh, how she wanted him to open his eyes. The blood seeping through the sheet alarmed her, and his coughing brought an even greater agony to his face. Adeline inwardly chastised herself for wanting to see his eyes, when he was obviously in so much pain.

"Mr. Lee, let me get you some water. You need to relax. Please, breathe deeply if you can. You have a very serious wound to your stomach, and a rib has also been fractured. It might hurt to breathe deeply, but please try."

"You're not going to leave me in here all by myself are you? Please, I'll stay in bed. Just talk to me. Just don't leave."

"Okay, Lieutenant, I won't leave. How about if I read to you?" The last thing she wanted to do was talk to him about anything personal. Adeline spied the book she had been reading to him earlier and continued to prattle on about it instead of what was really in her heart.

"Lieutenant Lee, did you know that one of the Brontë sisters, Emily, felt forced to write *Wuthering Heights* under a pseudonym? Yes, I believe the name was Ellis Bell, more of a manly name. I think it's a shame women can't be taken as seriously as their male counterparts, but at least the world knows it now, thanks to her sister Charlotte, who had the book published posthumously giving Emily credit."

"Ah, this is my favorite book. Heathcliff is my ideal image as a man, and Catherine is my ideal woman," Lieutenant Lee said as he looked Adeline in the face as if he didn't want to miss a single word she read.

"It's my favorite, also," she replied, and then Adeline began reading where she had left off; Isabel was telling Catherine that she was in love with Heathcliff, and if she would just stay out of the way, then maybe he would realize that he loved her, too.

Adeline read on and on. She was at the final sentence before she knew it. Lieutenant Lee said it aloud with her, and she looked up into his eyes. They were dark brown, almost black, and not much different from the dilated black pupil-filled ones that she had seen when he had first looked into her eyes. Now they were somehow far more expressive. It seemed that they could see right through Adeline to her inner being.

Adeline felt as if she were suddenly stark naked. It was very unsettling. She didn't want him to know how unsettled she was, so she kept staring at him until his mouth began to quirk in one corner and he said, "Are we having a staring contest?"

Adeline looked away, embarrassed, and replied rather flatly, "No…"

She tried to think of something witty to put him in his place. When she could think of nothing, she simply said, "No," again.

His expression quickly sobered and he mumbled, "Sorry."

Adeline checked the time; it was well past five o'clock. She had been in there for five hours! She was a little startled, and she must have said something aloud in her astonishment because Mordy inquired, "Something wrong?"

"No, I just didn't know that I had been in here this long."

"Really, well how long have you been up here?"

"Five hours," Adeline replied, still astounded.

"I suppose you had better check on the others. I appreciate your staying here and reading to me. I really am tired." Adeline could tell that he meant it, yet he hoped that she would stay.

In spite of her better judgment, Adeline asked, "Do you want me to stay until you go to sleep?"

He looked relieved. "If you don't mind, I would appreciate it."

"I did promise to take care of you." *Why did she have to say that out loud?* She shuddered.

"Yes, you did," he paused for a moment and then asked, "and how did you come to be a nurse in this God-forsaken war?"

"I was already nursing in Nashville, when my father died trying to protect our home and my mother. My mother's brother, my Uncle Rial, insisted we remove ourselves immediately to Cedarvine. Dr. Jennings is their son, and therefore, my cousin. Soon after, I nursed in Murfreesboro, but when my mother became ill, I came back to care for her. She died, but before my grief could even take hold, my Uncle Rial died, too. His death brought Phillip back then, and I've been helping him ever since." Adeline hadn't meant to divulge that much, but he had sounded so sincere in his inquiry that she felt compelled to give him the extended version.

"I'm glad you did come. Who else would have kept me such good company?" He sounded tired. Adeline wanted to hold his hand, so she took it as though she was going to check his pulse. When Adeline went to lower it, he gently took her hand in his and fell to sleep holding it. Adeline didn't want to leave, but she knew that she must. She put his hand beside his body and pulled the covers up under his chin.

With new resolve, Adeline came downstairs the next morning determined to be nothing more than a nurse to Lieutenant Lee. As she entered his room, she said, "Morning, Lieutenant Lee. How did you rest?"

She *was* going to treat him like any other patient. Upon returning to her room upstairs after the nightly rounds, Rebecca addressed her concerns about showing favoritism to a particular patient to Adeline. She had even gone so far to suggest that perhaps Adeline was falling in love with him. That nonsense had to be put to rest, thought Madeline. There were no such feelings, and she didn't want anyone, least of all Lieutenant Lee, to think that she was.

"Pretty well, actually."

"Good because we are going to check your wound and see how it is healing. If everything goes well, and an infection doesn't start, then you will be up and walking in no time."

"I'm ready when you are. Say, you never did tell me what your name was."

"My name is Miss Adeline," she informed him with no emotion in her voice. Then, she started to remove the bandage covering his wound.

"How many times do you have to change those bandages anyway?"

"I have to change them daily in order to avoid infection. You still aren't out of the danger zone yet. I want you to stay in bed. The doctor will determine how you are progressing. If you try anything drastic now, the sutures might pull, and we'll have to go through the healing process all over again."

She washed the wound, and he didn't even make a sound. He just stiffened when it began to sting. Just to keep conversation going in a professional manner she said, "We'll begin to stand you up and let you walk around the room in a week."

"Do I have to wait that long? I feel wonderful, I promise."

"You may feel *wonderful* now, but it would be really painful if you were to pull the sutures out. Promise me you won't try anything foolhardy to jeopardize yourself," Adeline demanded the promise in earnest. She hoped he didn't notice, and if he did, she hoped he would think it was the concern of a nurse for her patient.

❧   ❧   ❧

April 22, 1864

Lieutenant Lee is recovering as well as we all can hope. I'm having these feelings about him, and I've barely known him a week. I've tried to fight it. I guess I will have to face the inevitable. I am not ready!!! I'll fight it. Rebecca says that you can't fight your feelings; you have to face them and know them for what they are. But I am not ready...

Lieutenant Lee has told me that his family has put pressure on him. They want him to live up to his third cousin's, General Lee's, reputation. He says that he fights so hard on the battlefield to relieve himself of the pressure that he feels. He says that the relief is only momentary but any relief is better than none...tomorrow, maybe we can get him up and walking.

❧   ❧   ❧

It was difficult to get him standing, but they managed it. He was still a little sore and wobbly on his feet.

"Now, let's get you walking around the room a bit, and then I'll wheel you around the infirmary and give you the grand tour. Then I'll take you out on the grounds for a bit of fresh air. You look too pale. Maybe the sun will do you some good. It's a beautiful day, and I don't want to be cooped up in here when spring is in full bloom."

For the next hour, they exercised his muscles. By the end of the session he was tired, and his gait became halting. The next routine would take place outside so that they would have more room to move around. Adeline sat him down in the wheel chair when they had finished and said, "If you're not too tired, shall we go and take that tour?"

"Are there other patients in here other than myself?"

"Yes, just two others presently. There are two privates. You shall meet them later. Right now I want to show you some of the downstairs. Let's begin in the foyer at the piano."

"Did you say piano?" He looked really interested.

"Yes...why? Do you play?"

"Yes, I love piano music. I'm afraid I'm a bit rusty. Can you play?"

"Of course, my mother wouldn't have had it any other way. Two lessons a week since I was six."

"Will you play for me?"

"If you promise to be a good patient from now on, I'll do it."

He looked at her amused and said, "On my honor."

They walked slowly from the room into the foyer. "The piano is just below the staircase here." He sat down on the sturdy brocaded-covered bench before the piano and ran his hands over the keys as if greeting an old friend.

"What would you like me to play?" she asked as she slipped in beside him.

"Anything that strikes your fancy." Adeline could tell that as long as he could hear the sound again, he was content.

Following their "piano recital" and their walk in the garden, they had many more such occasions, and playing the piano became their favorite repast. Weeks went by, and as hard as Adeline tried not to care for this man, she was getting attached to him. Even though her brain tried to deny it, her heart seemed to plow through and take over in spite of everything. "I just hope that his name will never need to be added to the long list of lost souls on the wall…

CHAPTER 6

Cedarvine Manor, April 2003

"Believe when you lie. You will never need to recognize yourself. To Deceive..." Alchemy shifted as she came down the country road, allowing the loud sound of Disturbed, her favorite band, to blast through her car. She was excited to be able to spend the time with her grandfather. He was a genuine friend to her. As she sat in the big overstuffed orange chair, a vague memory of times spent there with her mother reading to her and her grandfather laughing made her eyes mist over with tears. She shook her head to rid herself of the memory.

She still watched in wonder as Cedarvine Manor came into view. She loved the old white plantation house with all her heart. It had always felt more like home. She hated her relatives who were trying to make Grandpa Leo sell his beloved house.

As she pulled into the driveway, she eyed the dark green two-door Ford Explorer with suspicion. *Who in the world was here?* Dad hadn't said anything about someone being here when he called last night. She missed her dad, but she had gotten used to his job keeping him out of town. That's why she and Leo had such a special relationship. They always had. Sometimes he was her mother and father all rolled into one special person. Her thoughts came back to the unknown car. Maybe a visitor? Shutting off the car, she reached in the backseat and grabbed her red duffel bag and her CD case before she shut the door. Pocketing her keys, she walked to the front door. As she entered, Alchemy set her duffel and CD case on the floor next to a small table.

"Grandpa Leo, I'm here!" Alchemy called into the house. She received no answer, so she called out again. This time she was answered by a loud crash.

Raising her eyebrows in alarm, she ran toward the sound. What she found was not what she was looking for. Instead of thinking she'd find her grandpa on the floor, a woman covered in flour greeted her.

"Who in the world are you, and why are you covered in flour?" Alchemy asked looking at the woman strangely.

"Who am I?" the woman asked, nonplussed. "Who are you?"

"This is my granddaughter," Leo's voice said from the other doorway.

"Grandpa!" Alchemy cried out like a little child who had just received an unexpected gift.

"Alchemy, how are you, my dear?" Leo replied, giving his favorite grandchild a bear hug.

"Grandpa, who in the world is this lady?"

"She's my in-home nurse. Your aunt and uncle sent her here to watch over me." His tone implied he certainly had no need of a nurse.

"Well, I'm sorry you feel that way, and I'm sorry I've created quite a mess here. I was looking through the cupboard to make us some tea, and when I reached into the cabinet, this canister fell, spilling most of its contents on me. If you'll excuse me, I'll go clean up and then come back down and straighten up the mess I've made," the woman said. "And by the way, my name is Madeline." With that she left the room, leaving a silly-looking swirl of flour dust in her wake.

Alchemy smirked as she watched the woman walk away. Leo's attitude rubbed off on Alchemy, and she dismissed Madeline with a turn of her head. She looked at her grandfather and said, "Come, Grandpa. Tell me what has been going on the past few days." She led her grandfather toward the living room.

Madeline shook her head as she swept up the stairs to her room and the connected bathroom. She couldn't believe that his granddaughter had almost laughed at her. She was trying to be nice and do something to soothe the irascible Leo's attitude when she had dropped the flour. She closed her bedroom door and stripped off her clothes. Walking into the bathroom, she took a quick shower, dressed, and then pulled her long flame-red hair into a ponytail. Several of the shorter strands fell in pieces around her pale face. Checking her reflection in the mirror, she hoped that her ice-blue eyes gave nothing away of what she was feeling, and smiling weakly to herself, she gathered her confidence and left her room.

She found Alchemy and Leo in the living room listening to rock music and talking. She had to say that his granddaughter looked nothing like the rest of the family. Her hair was black with neon pink streaks. She was wearing a pair of faded, ripped jeans and a black baby tee with a hot pink logo across the chest. Over that, she wore a black blazer with a strange symbol on the back. Both her ears were pierced several times, and she seemed totally at ease with her grandfather talking about everyday things. She looked completely out of place sitting with her grandfather in the clean living room in her grungy clothing.

"Ah, Nurse Madeline, I see that you have decided to join us," Leo said breaking his ongoing conversation with his granddaughter.

"Yes, well, I'm going to go clean up the mess in the kitchen," she said leaving the two to their conversation.

Alchemy watched Madeline leave the room. She was surprised to see such electric-blue eyes with the flame-red hair. That was a complete and total contrast from the woman who had just been covered in flour. Her posture was straight as a rod, and she seemed confident and at ease in moving through the house.

"I'm going to go help Madeline. I'll be back," Alchemy said to her grandpa and left him sitting in his chair, listening to the new Chevelle CD.

Alchemy walked into the kitchen to see Madeline sweeping up the flour. She stood there for a moment watching her.

"Are you going to just stare at me?" Madeline questioned not looking at Alchemy.

"I am going to help you," Alchemy flippantly said as she walked into the kitchen and picked up a washcloth.

"I don't need your help," Madeline responded firmly but politely. Alchemy had the urge to snap at the woman, but she refrained, knowing all too well that Grandpa Leo would be disappointed in her. Her mouth had gotten her in trouble more than once. "I said I was going to help you. Now, let me do it."

It seemed as if Madeline contemplated for a moment whether or not to let her help, but she must have finally given up that battle because she handed Alchemy a washcloth. Smiling at her, Alchemy set to cleaning the counters, while Madeline did the floors; they barely spoke to each other. Finally, Alchemy became bored with the silence.

"So, Nurse Madeline, how long have you been a home-care nurse?"

"A few years now," Madeline lied, "and please, just call me Maddy."

"Cool," Alchemy said, easily taking in Madeline's lie.

"Alchemy, I know this isn't what your grandfather wants, but I really do want to help him. Let's be friends. I can see that you care deeply for your grandfather."

"All right, Maddy," Alchemy agreed.

"So, Alchemy, how old are you?"

"I'm seventeen."

"That's great. I can't remember when I was seventeen," Maddy replied smiling.

"Yea, sometimes I wonder at how time flies."

"So what grade are you in? What high school do you attend?"

"I'm a senior at Wilson Central High School."

"It must be fun. It being your senior year and all."

"Loads, if you want to consider the dress code. And all of the other crap they put us poor students through," Alchemy said doing a fake faint to the floor. She knew she was being overdramatic, but Alchemy was good at being overdramatic. Her snobby relatives were good at that, too.

"I suppose those streaks are dress code," Maddy said motioning towards Alchemy's neon pink streaks.

"Oh no; I'd get trouble for them. We're on break right now, so I'm safe. Otherwise, I just put them in on the weekend," Alchemy said cleaning the washcloth.

Alchemy smiled at the memory of her aunt's overreaction to her attire at last year's family Thanksgiving dinner. Alchemy had strolled into the house wearing a pair of slightly baggy flare army green pants adorned with chains, black leather-studded pyramid belt, an extra belt around her hip, and a heartagram belt buckle. Her top was black and very nice with a scooped neck and red skull and tribal details. Her shoes had been the same chunky boots she was wearing now. Her hair, which was black, lacked the pink streaks she had now, but at that time were electric blue. It had been in a straight hairstyle. She had all her earrings in, each one or the other either gauged, silver studded, or black studded. Around her neck she wore a heartagram necklace. Her wrists had been adorned with black, red, silver, and blue gummy bracelets and also a studded wristband. Her makeup and nails had been heavy on the black. It had been chilly that day, so she was also wearing her prized fabric hooded trench coat.

Her relatives being the "people" they were called her a devil worshipper. She wasn't though; she actually went to youth group every Wednesday. She had laughed at them, along with her father and Grandpa Leo. She had argued with her cousin Brittany about her Gothic clothing. Her dad had asked her to stop, but the argument had escalated, and her aunt, well her aunt had tried to slap her. Her dad had stopped Aunt Melissa's arm before her hand could collide with her face, and after that the whole scene turned into a farcical charade of outrage by the prim and proper Aunt Melissa whose daughter only wore the preppy style of the Barbie dolls at her school. She remembered Grandpa Leo trying not to laugh, but he hadn't succeeded. He was laughing so hard, tears had fallen from his eyes.

Alchemy smiled once again at the memory.

"What are you smiling about?" Maddy questioned.

"Just a Thanksgiving dinner coming to an abrupt halt," Alchemy stated tossing the washcloth into the sink.

"We're done."

"Hallelujah!" Alchemy cheered jumping up and down.

"What is all the excitement about?" asked Leo as he hobbled into the kitchen. Seeing Alchemy laughing and smiling approvingly at his nurse, he decided he might take the high road for the time being.

"It's clean," Alchemy shouted falling to the floor in a dramatic antic. All three of them laughed as Alchemy picked herself up off the floor. Looking at the clock, Leo let them know his desire to have dinner.

"Let's go out," Alchemy offered.

"That's a great idea," Leo agreed. Maddy just nodded and disappeared to get her keys.

Alchemy sat in her dark purple room staring at the posters on the wall listening to a mixed CD. "Let Me Go" by 3 Doors Down was playing, and she was singing softly along with the music, thinking about the day's events. She had enjoyed their dinner out, and it felt good just talking and being with her grandfather. She loved him so much. While she and her grandfather chatted, Maddy had remained silent. She spoke a few words at a time, never interjecting, and only spoke when asked a question. When Maddy and her grandfather were speaking, Alchemy studied Madeline.

On the outside stood a proud woman who looked as if she knew what she had to do. Her posture was ramrod straight, and when she ate, she ate methodically, only taking a few bites at a time. More than just refinement ran through Maddy's veins. Her flame-red hair was pulled back in a high ponytail, the lush curls falling down her back. When certain light hit it, it looked like real fire. Liquid fire. She was wearing a pair of faded blue jeans, a blue T-shirt and a pair of blue and white tennis shoes. She sat across from them, but it was as if she was somewhere else. Alchemy had a feeling Maddy was hiding something, but she wasn't quite sure. Every time Madeline looked at Leo, her eyes seemed to fill with something that caused her to look away. Tomorrow she would find some time to talk to Maddy. Maybe even show her the writing on the wall. If she opened up, maybe Maddy would, too. Sliding down between the cool sheets of her bed, Alchemy turned out the lights and went to sleep.

The next morning, sunlight hit Alchemy's face. Groaning, she threw off the covers and crawled from the bed like a slug. She was not a morning person. And today was like any other day, except that today was like a Saturday because she was on break, and she was up at what time?? Looking over at the clock, she groaned again. It was eight o' clock in the morning. She hated when she woke up, and she didn't *have* to get up.

"Get up, A.J.," her grandfather said knocking on the door. Alchemy smiled at the nickname. Standing for Alchemy Jade, she remembered when her grandpa had started calling her that. It had been her tenth birthday, and she had decided she no longer liked her name. She wanted to be called A.J. because her favorite Backstreet Boy had been A.J. Every girl had her boy-band stage. She had thought it was the coolest thing that her name came out A.J., just like his did.

"I'm up, unfortunately," Alchemy whined wishing she could sleep longer. Trudging to the bathroom connected to her room, she took a shower, standing under the spray of hot water. Getting out, she dressed and towel dried her hair and pulled a brush through it. Snatching a black beanie off her dresser, she pulled it on her head, grabbed her iPod, and left her room. As she walked downstairs, the wonderful aroma of French toast, eggs, and bacon assaulted her.

"I know Grandpa can't cook. It has to be Maddy," Alchemy said, walking into the dining room to see her grandpa drinking coffee and reading the newspaper.

"You're right," Leo agreed. Alchemy set her iPod down on the table and walked into the kitchen. Saying good morning to Maddy, who was busy making French toast, she walked to the fridge and pulled out a can of coke. Popping the lid, she walked back into the dining room to sit next to her grandpa.

"Is that all you ever drink?" he questioned her.

"Yep," Alchemy said taking a drink.

"I've read that all that sugar's not good for you. I'm going to stop buying it for you. You need something healthier in the morning." Rolling her eyes at her grandfather, Alchemy placed the earphone of her iPod in her right ear, so she was still able to talk to her grandpa. A few moments later, Maddy placed the food down in front of them.

"Leo, after you're finished, I'll help you get ready," Maddy said before taking a drink of her coffee.

"Get ready? Get ready for what? Where are you going, Grandpa?" Alchemy asked, almost choking on her coke.

"To the doctor's office. You know how those damn doctors can be," Leo complained.

"Yeah, I know, Grandpa." Alchemy knew that her grandpa hated the doctors. Well, more like he hated the way they told you what to do. As if you were stupid and didn't know how to follow directions.

"Do you want me to go with you?" Alchemy questioned.

"No. Why don't you stay here with Nurse Madeline? She could use some company other than me," Grandpa Leo said taking a bite of a piece of bacon.

"Are you sure, Grandpa? I don't want you to hurt yourself," Alchemy said finishing off her coke.

Maddy interrupted the exchange by saying, "Leo, I'll take you. That's part of my job."

"I'll be fine. Don't worry about me so much," Leo chastised her. "I need some time away from you women. I like seeing my friends when the Senior Citizen's van picks me up. Don't take that away from me, too. No offense, Nurse Madeline, but I really am capable of getting into a van without your help."

"All right, if you say so," Madeline smiled as Leo turned and left the kitchen.

About an hour later, Alchemy watched as her grandfather gingerly climbed the short stairs of the "Senior Citizens' Wagon" that took the seniors to the doctor for their appointments.

"Hey, Maddy, come sit with me," Alchemy said leaving the kitchen to go sit in the living room.

"All right," Maddy said coming to sit down next to her on the couch.

"So, Maddy, do you like the house?"

"From what I've seen, yes. Your grandfather just gave me a general tour. I don't really know any of the history," Madeline replied truthfully.

"Well, why don't I show you the house and tell you about some of the history," Alchemy said standing up.

"I'd like that," Maddy agreed. They walked up the curved stairway to the second floor.

"Well, let's see…where to start? This house was an infirmary and convalescent home during and after the Civil War, housing wounded soldiers of both sides. Many died before they arrived or died here in this very house. Dr. Jennings ran the infirmary and owned the house until his death, and then it was passed down to the next in line. He was a very religious man," Alchemy said walking down the always-dark hallway to the door at the end of the upstairs hall.

"Jennings? That's my father's first name," Madeline told Alchemy.

"Really? Cool…of course, that's not a real unusual name around Lebanon. There's tons of Jennings' here."

"Yes, you're right, but that seems a bit coincidental. By the way, how many soldiers and nurses were here?" Madeline questioned, intrigued at the information Alchemy was giving her.

"There were two nurses: Rebecca, an older woman, and Adeline, cousin to Dr. Jennings, and it's hard to know how many soldiers there were. This is what I've gathered from reading old journals which I've discovered in some of the old unused rooms up here." They entered Madeline's room, and Alchemy reached up for an old picture. It was a picture of a soldier and a nurse. She handed Madeline the picture, who held it with special care.

"Is that Adeline?" she questioned pointing to the younger of the two nurses.

"Yea, that's Adeline. She was a stubborn one, with her fiery red hair and crystal blue eyes. At least that's how Mordy described her."

Just like me. "And who is Mordy?"

"Mordy was one of the soldiers. He loved Adeline," Alchemy said looking at the picture. "Wait a minute; she looks like you."

"No, she doesn't," Madeline denied it, but her hands were shaking slightly. Madeline was still startled by the similarities between herself and this woman.

To distract Alchemy, she once again asked, "Now, who was Mordy?"

"Actually, his name was Jacob, but he is Mordecai to me. He was a soldier who died in the house. He and Addie were in love."

"Addie? And how in the world do you know that they were in love?" she asked.

"Addie is Adeline for short. And the writing on the wall told me," Alchemy answered.

"The writing on the wall?" Madeline said trying to control her nerves and shaking hands. She was still startled by the picture.

"Yea, it's in the room at the end of the hall, next to Grandpa's old office. Here, let me show you," Alchemy said, walking out of the room. She went first to her bedroom and grabbed a ring of old skeleton keys.

Madeline followed Alchemy out of the room and down the hall. She watched as Alchemy stopped in front of the door, picked one of the keys from the ring, and inserted it in the door. Alchemy looked back at Madeline and then turned the key in the lock. The sound of the door unlocking made a loud click through the empty hall, and the door creaked loudly as she opened it. Madeline watched as Alchemy pushed open the door, and as she disappeared inside, Madeline reluctantly followed. She entered the dust-blanketed room and sneezed, the musty smell assaulting her nostrils. The room was dark; she had just adjusted to the darkness when Alchemy pulled open the dark curtains covering the window, sending piercing light into the room.

The room was vacant except for an old chair, worn with age. The pine walls were covered in old-fashioned-looking writing.

"What happened in this room?" Madeline questioned.

"I didn't bring you in here to tell you what happened in this room but to show you what is in this room," Alchemy stated.

She stared at the words before her. She gazed intently on the writing. There were names, letters, dates, and what appeared to be Bible verses.

"What are all of these?"

"Names of soldiers who were in this house."

Madeline's attention was caught by a particular message. It was a particularly emotional message, even though it was short and signed *Adeline*.

"Is this the same Adeline you were talking about earlier?"

"I think it must be."

"So, she was in love with this man," Maddy pointed out, even though she knew that answer.

"Yes, or what I've read in the journals anyway."

"Journals?"

"Yes, the journals that I found. They provided me with a lot of information that went on in this house when it was used as an infirmary and convalescent home," Alchemy said as she stared at the writing on the walls.

"Tell me more," Maddy said as she stared at the walls. "I want to know."

CHAPTER 7

Cedarvine Manor Convalescent Home, April 22, 1864

Mental status:	*Unknown. May be experiencing minor battlefield trauma; the patient's hand shakes mildly, and he complains of frequent nightmares.*
Physical status:	*Stable. The Bullet entered through the lower abdomen; upon striking a rib, both the rib and the bullet shattered. All locatable metal fragments have been removed; however, possibility of infection if the wound is not cleaned regularly. The patient is mobile and allowed up to 4 hours out of bed if assisted.*
Nurse on duty:	*Miss Adeline*

Dr. Jennings put down his pen and sighed deeply as he closed the inkwell. This one was strong, he thought to himself. Lieutenant Jacob Mordecai Lee had recently arrived from a nearby field hospital in Murfreesboro. Caught in an obscure skirmish, he'd told the doctor, although he had his doubts. A local rumor held that a Confederate lieutenant, leading his own band of sharpshooters, had been harassing Union supply lines for months; from the frightened Union men Dr. Jennings had treated, this lieutenant sounded like some kind of monster. Furthermore, the story went that the lieutenant was seen being helped away from a furious firefight about a month before; it just so happened to be the same day the lieutenant claimed to have been hurt.

Nevertheless, he couldn't blame him for keeping to himself; he'd had a horrendous time simply staying alive. The field hospital he'd been in was nothing more than a collection of tents and unskilled civilians desperately trying to save lives. Lieutenant Lee's wound hadn't even been looked at when he had been transferred to Cedarvine, and Dr. Jennings had to perform a risky maneuver just to prevent infection. The fact that he was still breathing shocked the doctor even now. His medical knowledge couldn't explain it, but his Bible could; *God has a purpose for him.* Dr. Jennings gently uttered his favorite saying. "Miracles happen under the most unusual circumstances; it's just a matter of recognizing them."

He perused his office as he gave an airy groan of relaxation. The black oak of his desk seemed to rise seamlessly from the similar shade of wooden board that covered the floor. The wallpaper in this part of the house was slightly worn and cracking in the corners; several aged paintings tempered the otherwise barren walls. An unusually ornate fireplace adorned the back wall; this had been the master bedroom, curiously placed at the back of the house. The portrait of his great-grandfather hung over the fireplace warming the room with its deep smile. He had been doctor, too, or at least he had tried; medical practice back then was less than sturdy, not like the advanced science it was in Dr. Jennings' day. People said they looked alike, Dr. Jennings and his father, and apart from the hazel of Dr. Jennings' eyes and the lack of grey in his beard, they could have been brothers. Hardly encouraging, Dr. Jennings thought, seeing as he had been hung by a mob for consorting with British officials. That was years ago, however, practically another age; the British hadn't set foot in America for over fifty years. Now, this country had its own conflict, a grand struggle on an almost personal level. Brother versus brother, fighting back-to-back and then suddenly against one another, tables turning rapidly, and fatality everywhere. The life of a doctor was trying.

Suddenly, he remembered the time of day, and hastily checked his pocket watch. Mr. Easting, the owner of the general store, would be arriving with his weekly supplies in scarcely an hour. If he meant to get anything done, now was the time. He began riffling through the papers on his desk, opening and closing drawers, lifting manuals and books. The rattle of brass handles on oak accompanied his hunt. Ducking down to reach the bottom drawer, Dr. Jennings muttered to himself as the office door creaked open; he continued searching.

"Sir? Can I help?" came the light lilting of a young boy's voice.

"No, thank you, my boy. Eh, on second thought, have you seen my Bible?"

"No, sir. That middle drawer, on the left, isn't that where you keep it?"

The drawer came loose and crashed to the floor, medical reports falling in a great mess that threatened to flood the room. Hidden beneath a stack was his old, leather-bound, dog-eared Bible.

"Ah, why thank you! You've always been a useful lad for keeping an old mind sane." A colossal smile spread across his face and infected the young lad with a soft grin. His blue eyes twinkled radiantly; it was rare to see him this happy. With his glasses tipped down, Dr. Jennings sternly gazed at him over the oval rims; Nicholas knew the look and took a guilty posture.

"I hope you've done your daily readings…ah, of course you haven't. Well, come then, off to your room and read Psalms 11. And after that, would you mind preparing the stables; Mr. Easting will be here soon, and the least we can do is keep him for supper." He ran off, his blonde hair flashing as he pounced deftly out the door, the slap of his sandals fading in the distance.

"Ah, poor Nicholas—the eternal orphan."

Dr. Jennings had found him in Kentucky, the drummer boy for a company of Union militia. It was an odd gathering of uncouth frontiersmen, one in which the lad hardly fit. He was scarcely twelve when the company was sent into a skirmish, wiped out, obliterated before his eyes. Dr. Jennings was there, working in the field hospital. His assistant nurse had been wounded while running errands, and there, leaning against a withered oak, was the weeping child. Dr. Jennings thought nothing of it and asked for his help with binding a leg wound; he stood stock straight, and gazed at him for a hard moment before setting to the task with such a will as Dr. Jennings had ever seen. All that long, gloomy day, they worked, as Dr. Jennings taught him the rougher tasks of sewing wounds, performing unbearably messy operations, and severing gory limbs. That night, he slept like the dragon sleeps beneath the mountain, and awoke ready to breathe life back into the injured men he watched over. Dr. Jennings learned much of this boy through his subsequent actions. He was gentle in composure; his manner in dealing with the unruly was smooth and consoling. Nicholas somehow felt for them in a deeper sense; he helped them bear the pain, understanding better than anyone that in order to heal the wound, sometimes one had to "hurt" them to make the healing go faster. He could be clumsy at times; occasionally his stitching was awry, or he would perhaps wrap the wound at an awkward angle, although this was certainly understandable when one considers the abruptly minimal training he had received. He worked wonders on patients' minds and souls, and many a hardened face was softened by his reassuring grin.

Although Dr. Jennings was only an interim doctor, he had worked in Kentucky a full year before his replacement arrived in late 1863. With him came a letter from Dr. Jennings' family in Tennessee saying his father was extremely ill, and his presence was needed immediately. Although the majority of his life had been spent in the North, he always maintained strong ties with his Southern relatives.

He heard little Nicholas' voice ringing in his ears as he remembered the moments he spent preparing for his hasty departure. Nicholas was to be reassigned to another company soon; drummer boys were in short supply in those brutal years.

"Sir…your Bible, Sir. You left it in the medical supplies tent." He handed Dr. Jennings the book, holding it out with his slender fingers. He packed the last of his field kit and placed it next to the bundle of clothing by his side. Dr. Jennings reached out for the Bible but caught Nicholas' eye at the last moment. In his eyes was an unbound reverence for Dr. Jennings; somehow, having this child's respect was infinitely more meritorious than having the calm admiration of a thousand fellow colleagues. Dr. Jennings knew that Nicholas must come with him. With a gracious smile, he pushed the heavy book back into Nicholas' hands.

"Keep it, lad. Where we're going, only Christ can help us rebuild our lives." Within the hour, Dr. Jennings had secured Nicholas' release; he would go with him to Tennessee.

Dr. Jennings thought back to the times before he had arrived in Nashville the last time. His father, Rial C. Jennings, had married Phillip's mother and moved south before the war. He was one of the few rich men in Nashville who hadn't been a plantation slaver and, thus, was worth infinitely more because his money was in the bank, not the fields. He'd started construction on his own mansion in 1832 but never seemed to be able to finish it. Dr. Jennings had been in medical school, abroad, and in the North for many years when he received word that his mother had died. That was 1859; worried about his father, he convinced his father that he ought to return, if only to be at his mother's funeral. With her death, Phillip's father seemed frustrated and lonely, but rather than allow him to visit more often, he pushed him away, insisting that he could do more in the world if he stopped worrying about his father's health. When the war started in 1861, Dr. Phillip Jennings was again compelled to return home to his aging father, but he pressed his son to put himself to good use as an army doctor; after all, he was one of the few qualified doctors who did not have a permanent position. Phillip humored his father's request, but only after he was sure he would have good company. Phillip asked his father's widowed sister and her daughter, Adeline, to stay with him at the mansion. They consented, chiefly because they needed someplace to stay when Adeline's father had been killed during the war. Last Phillip had heard, Adeline was nursing soldiers in Murfreesboro.

In late 1863, a mere five months ago, Dr. Jennings arrived at his father's mansion amid sheer chaos. He and Nicholas stepped out of the wagon into the late Tennessee chill of early morning. He was awed by the size of the mansion, and it looked quite complete, a drastic improvement over the last time Phillip had seen it. The porch was a flurry of activity and voices. A crowd of people, most of whom were relatives or lawyers, gathered around a woman with fiery red hair; she was trying desperately to be heard above the crowd. Dr. Jennings recognized her instantly, despite the fact that he had only met her twice before. He boldly walked through crowd, parting the ocean of tacky suits and Southern drawl.

"Miss Adeline, is there a problem here?" he inquired loudly. Her face lit up; the crowd began grumbling and chattering in quiet whispers. She stumbled over her words in hesitation.

"Phi...Dr. Jennings! You came! Eh, these people are all..."

"Adeline, just what in heaven's name is going on here?" he looked around carefully before proceeding, and a feeling of dread came over him. "And where...where is my father?" The crowd was instantaneously hushed.

Adeline's face already held the answer.

"Doctor, your father is...deceased. He went peacefully, quickly even! The pneumonia struck about three months ago; it was the wint-" But Dr. Jennings was already moving. Climbing the porch stairs with haste, he turned around with a dramatic twist. With complete solemnity, he suppressed his emotions and handled the situation the way any good doctor does.

"And then I suppose you are all here for the house, the inheritance? What did you think, that his son wouldn't return? Well, I'm here now." He felt enraged, all at once. "*I'm here now!*"

The crowd stood in silence, a shocked silence that seemed to carry on into perpetuity. Slowly, one or two of them came to, and went back to their usual grumbling as they turned and made off. Within the hour, all were gone, and not another word was spoken on the matter.

At first, things between Adeline and Dr. Jennings were hard. Her mother, Dr. Jennings' aunt, had died of pneumonia shortly before his father had succumbed. Adeline had spent her time nursing, something she knew would take her mind from her grief; after all, war was a time for self-sacrifice. They spent the first few weeks pulling their lives together; the house was in mild disarray, and they both had commissions to attend to.

Adeline and Dr. Jennings felt lost. With their parents gone, an enormous mansion in their possession, and death and pain all around, they decided to do what they knew best. Dr. Jennings sent a letter to the bank, asking them to send the bulk of his father's money, the rightful inheritance that the relatives had been after; he wrote letters to army contacts requesting any available medical supplies, for which he would willingly pay. Adeline wrote a letter to a friend she had worked with in Murfreesboro, and Rebecca arrived a few days later to work with them. An older woman, her children away fighting, they welcomed her experience.

Within a month of hard work, they had the house bustling efficiently as a convalescent home for those fortunate brave hearts who had escaped death in battle.

He sighed deeply; with a start, he remembered his restricted timetable and reached for his Bible. His age was catching up to him; his forgetful reminiscences were becoming more and more frequent. Sliding his chair back as he rose, he peered out the window at the glowing sun. The day looked lively, and he couldn't wait to escape into the refreshing air that he missed so much. He found all these reports and needless papers stifling. Moving out the door into the musky hallway, he vowed to greet the day on his terms.

CHAPTER 8

Cedarvine Manor, May 2003

Maddy was feeling very guilty for what she was doing. She hated feeling so deceitful. As she sat alone in her room, she had second thoughts racing through her head; after all, Leo and Alchemy really seemed to trust her.

Why did she ever agree to do this? Why would she do something so underhanded to someone who hadn't done anything to deserve it? She was really starting to like Leo, as stubborn as he was, and the spell of the house had been enveloping her since she arrived…she didn't want to see it torn down. She was trying to think of a good reason why or how she could get out of this without risking her father's wrath. Nothing that had even the slightest chance of working came to mind at the moment, and for some reason, she still didn't want to be a disappointment to her father. She had worked so hard just to please Jennings, despite the things with which she did not agree, though her efforts never seemed to be enough for him.

She felt so angry with herself but even more so at Ron. Somehow she just knew that he was behind her father's decision to put her in charge of getting this project finished. He should have known better than to put her in this kind of position. She was under his control, too, which was the way that he liked things, just like her father. She had never been able to stand up to either one of them, but she suddenly realized one thing…she *knew* she didn't love Ron and couldn't marry him. The other thing she knew for sure was that she didn't want to carry out this plan any more at all. She grabbed the cell phone out of her purse and dialed his number. She froze in hesitation and dread; she really didn't want to talk to him. What exactly was she going to say to him? That was just it; she didn't have much to tell him. She hadn't been trying too hard to talk to Leo about selling the house at all. She found it difficult to even bring it up to him. Every time she had tried, something inside her would not allow it. Ron and Maddy had barely spoken since the day that she canceled the wedding. She just knew that there would be awkwardness between them, but now she didn't care how awkward it might be. She finally got up the courage to press the "send" button. That was it; there was no backing down now.

After the first ring, Maddy was tempted to hang up, but she refrained, and after the second, Ron picked up the phone.

"Hello?" he answered.

"Ron? It's Maddy. I just wanted to talk to you about what I'm doing here."

"Okay, what's going on? How's the progress coming?" he replied, surprisingly very polite.

"Everything's just fine," she lied, "but…I don't think that what you're asking me to do is very fair. I mean, Leo can be such a nice man, and he just adores this house. Who could blame him; have you seen this place? It is worn but absolutely gorgeous! Besides, he's getting old, and he should be able to enjoy his home without being worried about losing it."

"I don't care how old the man is. That is none of my concern. The only thing that I can focus on is getting this done soon; the deadline is coming up. His family wants him to sell, too; they need the money to put him into a nursing home so that he's taken care of. I can't afford for you to get emotional, as you tend to do," he lectured.

"What are you implying with that kind of remark? I don't know what my emotions have to do with any of this situation. Why do you insist on being so insensitive all of the time?"

"Madeline, I was simply making a statement. What I meant by it was that if you aren't willing or can't do this job, I'm going to be forced to take action into my own hands, and I won't be as nice as you have been."

"I think that you're heartless for doing this. Anyone with a conscience would agree, but I guess you wouldn't know anything about that…would you?" accused Maddy.

"Can you just drop it already? I've tried to explain things to you, but you are too stubborn to even listen. Is this why you decided to call, to reprimand me and try to make me feel guilty?"

"No, I wasn't calling you for that. I wanted to speak to you, as my boss, because that's the only thing you are to me. This house has so much history, and I would hate to be involved in erasing it."

"I don't know why you are so against this. It's not like your history is being erased. This house has nothing to do with you. This has got to be done. Your father has given me strict orders, mind you. This will make us all very rich, and we're doing something good for the working people."

"I know, I know, it's got to be done for your benefit and his. Once again, you are the only ones who even matter at all. You two are one in the same, not caring that this man's home is being taken from him. Leo doesn't only think of it as just a home either; this place is everything to him. Maybe you think it has nothing to do with me," she said remembering the picture of the man and woman sitting on the porch swing, "but the moment that I was put into this house, that made it something. Also, unlike you, I actually care about things other than myself. I'm sure that this situation would be a lot different if it was your house being threatened," Maddy snapped at him.

"Good-bye, Madeline," Ron said to her. "I have a big agenda for today, and arguing with you is not part of it."

Maddy sat in her room, trying to calm herself. Her body was shaking in fury. She didn't want to be angry anymore. *I really wish that there was a way out of this. I have to figure something out, and fast, and there's not a whole lot of time.*

"I'm not going to let him bring me down. He's not worth my time or my energy," she spoke to the room. She started pacing around her room, taking deep breaths. She looked at her surroundings and began to feel a little better; this place seemed to do that to her. As she stood in silence, she started to think of the piano. She wanted to play it so badly. She immediately decided that she would. Maybe that was just the thing to bring her discordant thoughts into harmony; just being around a piano always seemed to work.

She walked out of her room, and there stood Leo with a questioning look upon his face. There was an uncomfortable silence between the two, so after a few moments, Maddy continued on her way to the piano. She needed time to relax herself, but now she was worrying about what part of her conversation had been heard.

"Things just keep getting worse for me," she mumbled to herself as she strolled through the hallway, heading to the stairs. She took each step slowly and smoothly, caressing the handrail as she moved downward. She made her way around the lower level until she finally came to the piano. It was so beautiful and so old. When she placed her fingers on the keys, she almost felt as if she had taken a step back into time. She closed her eyes and thought of the picture that Alchemy had shown her. She wanted to understand how and why that woman looked so much like her. It didn't make any sense at all.

Being in this house, surrounded by Leo and Alchemy who made her feel like part of the family made her wish that she knew something about her family's history, no matter how little there was to know. There had to be something, but what could it be?

She opened her eyes and glanced at the piano once again.

CHAPTER 9

Cedarvine Manor, October 5, 1864

"Good morning, boys! How is everyone doing today?" Adeline said as she entered the room.

"We're doing much better now that you're in the room, Nurse Adeline," one of the fallen soldiers said.

"You boys are sweet." As she moved beyond their beds and closer to Mordy's, she said, "And how is my favorite patient doing this morning?"

"Well, I'm feeling right as rain today, Miss Adeline," Mordy said.

"I told you to call me Adeline or Nurse Adeline. I don't like feeling like an old maid," Adeline responded.

"I'm sorry, Miss…I mean, Nurse Adeline, but every time I see you my heart starts to beat as if it is saying Adeline."

"I'm glad I make you feel that way." She turned away from him and said, "Now you boys finish your breakfast. The doctor will begin seeing you in just a moment."

Adeline climbed the sweeping staircase and went to the end of the hall where her cousin kept his office. "Doctor, the patients are nearly done with their breakfast. You can begin seeing them soon," Adeline said, standing in Dr. Jennings' doorway.

"Thank you, Adeline," Dr. Jennings said, still looking down at his stack of reports. "I'll begin checking on them soon."

"Phillip…well…you value my opinion, don't you? I mean, from a medical perspective."

"Why, yes, you've turned out to be useful in everything here, especially in some of the desperate situations we've encountered." He leaned forward, crossing his arms. "Why do you ask?"

Adeline fidgeted nervously.

"Phillip, you know Lieutenant Lee. He's having quite a time—getting better that is. His wound hasn't seemed to get much better in all this time, and…he still has night terrors about the war. I think…well, I know of your interest in the mind and such things. Could you spend some extra time with him, and see if there is anything more you think we can do?"

"Adeline, my dear. Why are you asking this of me?"

When Adeline opened her mouth, nothing but a long-winded babble came out.

"It's just that the nature of his wound is very dangerous. The chance of infection has always been high, and all I'm asking is that you examine him a little closer and make sure he's getting better. Perhaps we could move him to the room upstairs, the one we never use. It's got an extra mattress, and it would be easier to keep an eye on him." She ended with a quick puff of breath. She had forgotten to mention that this room was directly across from her own. Phillip was suspicious but didn't let it show.

"Adeline, if I showed special attention to one patient, I would have to show them all special attention," Jennings said. "I'm sorry, but I just can't do that. Procedure, you understand."

"But Ph…Phillip—" Adeline started.

"That's the end, Nurse Adeline. I won't do it. I just won't." And with that, he turned his attention back to his papers.

"Yes," said Adeline dejectedly. Before leaving the room, she turned back to him with an indignant twist of her hips.

"Phillip, do you always have to be so…so…" She searched for the right word, "Stuffy?!"

Dr. Jennings, obviously taken aback, raised his head slowly, adjusting his reading glasses carefully before proceeding. "Adeline, I'm simply doing what's best here. Don't pretend around me; I can see where this is going. You have feelings for this soldier, do you not? Ah—don't answer, because I can already see it written on your face. This once, you must take my word, and take it solemnly. Lieutenant Lee is a good man, but there's nothing but trouble in this. You know perfectly well that we are never to become attached to our patients.

Do you think I'm old-fashioned? Well, good. It makes my opinion all the more valid. You've had your share of heartbreak, and it's my responsibility to make sure you suffer no more."

Adeline held back a tear and bit her lip hard as she left the room. She knew he was right. Would she ever learn? She needed to shore up the breaches in her heart and get her mind back to the business of nursing. Her ramrod straight posture gave proof of her resolve. Adeline walked into the patients' ward and asked, "All finished with breakfast, boys? Then the doctor will see you all."

"Miss Adeline, why would a nice gal like you take care of a bunch of rough soldiers like us?" Mordy asked. "You should be out having a nice time."

"Well, Mordy," Adeline answered. "I would rather stay here and take care of soldiers than go out any day. Going out would just mean I'm far away from you fine gentlemen."

"But Miss Adeline, you deserve to go out and have some fun. We're soldiers. We'll be okay by ourselves."

"No, I would rather stay here, where I'm needed."

"All right, Miss Adeline, but one day when I'm well, I'm going to take you out as a gentleman should."

"Is that a promise, Mordy?"

"Yes ma'am. It sure is."

"Well, then, I'll keep it on my calendar," Adeline said. "Now, may I please continue my work?"

"Carry on, Miss Adeline."

Adeline went from room to room, turning down the beds and dusting anything that needed to be dusted. She helped Rebecca make and serve lunch. By one o'clock, she was feeling tired, but she knew that she had work to do. Dr. Jennings had examined all of the patients, and he had left the house to take his daily afternoon constitutional around the grounds of the manor. At 1:30, Rebecca came up to her and said, "Lt. Lee said that he wanted to ask you something."

"Oh, can't it wait? I still have to scrub the kitchen floor and empty the chamber pots," Adeline protested.

"Go on, dear. I'll take care of it. You go see what he wants," Rebecca advised.

Adeline walked into the patients' ward and saw that Mordy was the only one who was awake. "All right, Mordy. What do you need of me?" she asked.

"Well, Miss Adeline, you know how we've been taking walks in the garden. Well, today I thought maybe you could give me a tour of the house."

"What? Mordy I have too much work to do. Maybe another time, but not right now."

"Miss Adeline, my grandmother always said there's no time like the present. I'm sure Rebecca won't mind."

"He's right, dear," said Rebecca who stood in the doorway.

"Oh, all right. But Dr. Jennings cannot know about this. He doesn't like people going through his house like it's a museum."

Against her better judgment, and with little thought to the vow she had just taken to remain detached, Adeline supported Mordy as they began to slowly walk through her cousin's house together. As they walked, Adeline told Mordy that it was her Uncle Rial who originally owned the house, and Dr. Jennings had taken it over and turned it into a convalescent home after his father died. Once upstairs, Adeline and Mordy peeked in various rooms, but Adeline was nervous, not only because she was alone with Mordy, but because she knew how disappointed Phillip would be if he were to return and find them upstairs. As they reached the end of the hall by Phillip's office, they walked past a room where the door was slightly ajar. Mordy saw the shadow of a hospital bed and a single chair. He asked Adeline, "What's in that room?"

"That room is supposed to be locked," Adeline said.

"What's in there?" Mordy asked again.

"Nothing," Adeline lied. "Nothing is in there."

"It looks like a hospital bed was in there."

"I'm sorry, Mordy, but I can't take you in there."

"Why?"

"I'd rather not talk about it."

"Did something bad happen in there?"

"Sometimes…"

"Adeline, please tell me. I truly want to know."

"Mordy, that room is there so that none of the soldiers who died here are forgotten. Their bodies may die, but their souls live forever in these walls," Adeline proclaimed. "Oh, listen to me! It's not all morbid writing in there, Mordy. Some soldiers write their mama's name on the wall, some write Scripture, some write dates, some write remembrances…" she stumbled onward. "Mordy, can you promise me something?"

"Sure, Adeline. What is it?"

"Promise me that I won't see your name on these walls. Promise me that I won't have to come in here and write your name. Promise me…"

"Adeline," Mordy interrupted. "I promise you that you will never see my name on any on these walls. I'm going to stay with you."

She blushed at his words and quickly said, "Thank you, Mordy. I guess we really should get you back to bed." Adeline and Mordy carefully made their way back downstairs to the patients' ward, and Mordy carefully reclined on the bed.

"Miss Adeline, I want to thank you for showing me the house. Now I realize how much work you have to do just to keep the house clean."

"Thank you, Mordy. I'm glad you realize how important my job is and why I don't go out to have fun. Now you get some sleep."

"Yes ma'am," Mordy mumbled as he drifted off to sleep. Neither of them saw Phillip standing by the stairs, sadly shaking his head.

Later that afternoon, upstairs in her bedroom, Adeline wrote in her journal. As she poured her thoughts on the page she heard something drop outside her door. As she opened the door, she saw it was Nicholas, Dr. Jennings' helper.

"Nicholas, what are you doing up here?" Adeline asked. "Shouldn't you be helping Dr. Jennings?"

He was picking up medical items that had obviously fallen from the leather knapsack slung over his shoulder.

"I was, Miss, but he sent me up here to get something," Nicholas answered.

"What did he send you to get?" Adeline asked, wondering why Dr. Jennings didn't ask Rebecca or herself.

"Some new bandages and gauze for Lieutenant Lee, ma'am," Nicholas confirmed. "Dr. Jennings thinks that his infection might be coming back."

Adeline couldn't believe what she was hearing. "An infection? But how? Why? Nicholas what does Dr. Jennings mean by infection?" Adeline asked.

"Well, he said that Lieutenant Lee has a fever, and that most assuredly means infection, so he sent me to get some bandages and gauze to clean and rewrap his wound," Nicholas replied. "Is there anything else you want to know, ma'am?" he asked.

"No, Nicholas. Go about your chores," Adeline instructed. Though she wanted to rush to his side, she knew Phillip would disapprove, and though she wanted to cry, she knew that wouldn't do either one of them any good.

As she moved to the door, she said, "I can't let this get to me down. I have a job to do, and I know that Mordy will pull through this." She went downstairs and helped Rebecca make dinner.

"Are you feeling okay, Addie? You seem quiet and a bit pale," Rebecca prompted.

"I'm fine. I just have so much on my mind," Adeline replied.

"If you need to talk, you know I'm here to listen."

Adeline passed dinner out to the soldiers. When she finally got to Mordy's bed, she had calmed her nerves and steeled her face into a mask of professional efficiency. Although he looked flushed from the fever, he seemed agitated and jumpy.

"Adeline, I need to move. Do you think I could play the piano before dinner?" Mordy asked.

"Aren't you hungry?"

"Not really. I figured the men would like some music while they eat."

"Oh, I don't know, Mordy. You've already been out of bed today. I don't know if it's wise."

"Come on, Miss Adeline. Let him play," one soldier hollered.

"Yeah, I would enjoy some music with my meal," another agreed.

"Very well. He can play, but you're sitting in a wheelchair."

Adeline wheeled Mordy to the piano and said, "I'll be right back. I'm going to go get you some sheet music."

"I don't need any sheet music," Mordy said. "I play by ear."

"I'm getting sheet music, Mordy. We have some great songs," Adeline said.

"Oh, all right, but I get to pick what I play," Mordy said.

"Fine," Adeline agreed. "I'll be right back."

She skipped lightly up the stairs to get some sheet music out of what was at one time the music room of Rial's wife, but as Adeline passed Dr. Jennings' office, he called her in. "We need to talk," he said.

"About what, Doctor?" Adeline asked.

"About you disobeying me, that's what. I told you not to show other patients special treatment, and still you disobeyed my wishes," Dr. Jennings proclaimed.

"Phillip, I don't know what you're talking about," Adeline said. "Now if you don't mind, I was about to let Mordy play some music."

"I saw you with him, Adeline. Upstairs, showing him my private quarters. Adeline, you know that it is quite to the contrary of our duties to show affection toward a patient," Dr. Jennings said. With a huge sigh, Phillip added, "Adeline, I just don't want to see you get hurt again."

"Phillip, I am not going to get hurt again. Stop treating me like I'm a child. I love him," Adeline blurted out.

"Adeline, you don't know what you're saying. You only think you're in love. How do you know that he isn't already married? Or engaged?" Dr. Jennings asked. "You don't know anything about him."

"I know that I love him. And that he cares about me," Adeline said. "Now if you don't mind, *Doctor*, I have patients to look after."

Adeline stormed out of the room.

"Adeline, you're making a big mistake if you tell him that you love him," Dr. Jennings called out to her. "Don't be surprised when he breaks your heart. That's what soldiers do: break hearts and take lives."

Adeline walked back into the room, shaking. She looked flushed and on the brink of tears. Mordy looked at Adeline with concern.

"What's wrong? You couldn't find the sheet music?" he asked to defuse her obvious distress.

"I'm fine," Adeline lied. "But you know what? I think there's some sheet music right inside the piano bench."

Mordy lifted the brocaded-covered seat, and the hinges creaked a bit. He struggled to angle his wheelchair to scoop out the contents.

"Well, look what we have here, Miss Adeline! Why, there's a treasure trove in here. All kinds of sheet music. And look at this. It's a *Stephen Foster Songbook!*"

Are you sure you feel up to playing, Mordy? You don't want to overdo it."

"I'm fine, really. What shall we perform? How about 'Nothing But A Plain Old Soldier'? Or would you like to try 'Mary Loves the Flowers'? Here's 'Wilt Thou Be Gone Love?' That's one of my mother's favorites. Such a lovely duet she and my father used to sing to that song. Now, here's my favorite. 'Beautiful Dreamer.' Yes, this is the perfect song to play. Let's give it a whirl, then, and Adeline, sing along. I can only believe that you'll have the voice of an angel, too," Mordy whispered by her ear.

From the top of the curved staircase, Dr. Jennings looked down at the pair and said quietly, "This will not end well."

CHAPTER 10

Cedarvine Manor, May 2003

"This woman is up to something! There is something wrong. No one has ever had so much interest in this house," thought Leo. "Ms. Madeline is more concerned in this 'darn' house than me. There's something up, and I'm gonna' find out what."

He had gone up to the old storage room to find some papers for the insurance company, and as he shuffled through his old desk, he vowed to get to the bottom of Madeline's "interest" in his home. He, too, was interested in his house—in saving it! He started to go down the back stairs to the kitchen, when he heard the door to his old study creak open.

After a long, thoughtful time sitting at the piano, Madeline had gone back upstairs and headed to the old storage room. She knew she couldn't tell Leo about her plan to save the house, not just yet anyway. She was bound and determined to find some historic importance to this house so her father's company could not tear it down. She remembered a class she took about urban development while she was working on her engineering degree, and though then it meant nothing to her, she suddenly remembered something about preservationist laws designed to save historical buildings from urban blight. Since Alchemy and Leo had shared that Leo's office was a mess, not just a literal mess, but a mess of boxes containing old records dating back to the 1830s, she reasoned that there had to be something significant in the room. When she had seen the door was slightly cracked, she knew it was her chance to go in and start looking around. With all the old books and photographs and journals, certainly Leo *must* have something he didn't even know was important. She vowed to find something. She moved to Leo's desk and quietly opened the top left drawer.

Leo, at the top of the back staircase, heard the office door creak open. He quietly shuffled back to the open door.

"Can I help you with something?" Leo asked Madeline in an irritated tone.

Madeline jumped and gasped, "Oh, Leo, you scared me."

"Who else would you expect?"

"No one, I was just…" Madeline stammered.

"You were just snooping through my desk! What do you think I have in there? Important documents? A gun? What?" By the tone of his voice, she could tell Leo was becoming very agitated.

"I—I—I was just looking for a key to open the bathroom door in my room. I accidentally locked it, and I really need to get in…" Madeline had no clue what she was talking about or how the story she had just told Leo had miraculously flowed out of her mouth.

"Why would a key to your bathroom be in my desk in my storage room? Why would anyone keep a key to the bathroom in a storage room?" Madeline knew Leo suspected something was up.

"I'm sorry. I didn't know where else to look."

"No! I think you knew exactly what you were doing."

Everything was happening too fast for Madeline. Not knowing what to do, Madeline gulped out a murmured apology and ran from the room. In her room, she reviewed the embarrassing scene. Madeline was worried about how this would affect everything, including staying here. Would Leo demand she leave? What was she going to do? All the possibilities of what the outcome would be from this slip-up kept running through her head. What could she possibly tell Leo to explain her behavior? She finally came to the conclusion that it was time for her to leave before Leo forced her to leave.

Thinking about these things made Madeline anxious, and a terrible foreboding came over her. She started to cry, but knowing that wouldn't get her anywhere, she turned sharply to the right, like someone trying to shake away a bad dream. The sharp turn caused her to bump into the bookcase, and from the top tumbled an old leather-bound book. Startled, she bent to retrieve it. Her fingers left a perfect imprint on the dusty binding. She carefully blew the dust from the top and front and sat down slowly on her bed. The book seemed to open of its own accord to a yellowed page, and she started reading from it:

October 5, 1864

Today was such a wonderful day. Even though the doctor says that as a nurse I cannot get emotionally involved with a patient, I can't help it. When I am with him, he makes me feel happy. The war continues claiming victims. Even though Mordecai was badly wounded, he still has a beautiful spirit. Despite everything he has seen and gone through, he continues to smile and laugh about things…

Madeline continued to read until she heard a crash out in the hallway. It sounded like a box of heavy books had been thrown down the stairs. Rushing out of her room, she found Leo lying at the bottom of the first landing, unconscious. She flew down the stairs to the landing and cradled Leo's head on her lap. She checked for a pulse and felt hope when she found the pulse beating steadily. She pulled off the cardigan sweater she had been wearing over her blouse, folded it, and carefully placed his head on it. Madeline ran to the phone to call an ambulance.

"Things can't get any worse," thought Madeline while she waited on the phone for 911. Madeline was so frustrated with everything. Finally, someone at the end of the receiver picked up, "911 emergency!"

"Yes, my name is Madeline Hightower, and I'm caring for Leo Dunn at Cedarvine Manor out on Rt. 231 just past Couchville Pike. He just fell down the stairs, and he is unconscious! Please, we need an ambulance immediately!" Madeline cried.

"An ambulance is on the way, ma'am. Is he breathing?"

"Yes, his breathing is steady, but please hurry!" She rushed to the landing.

A short time later, she heard faint sirens in the distance. She ran frantically to open the door, and an EMT came bounding up the steps. "Where is he? How long has it been? Did you check for a pulse?" Another EMT rushed in with a stretcher. Everything was happening so fast. She directed them to the landing.

"Are you riding with us?" the first EMT asked.

"No," Madeline said. "I need to stay here and call his family…"

Before Madeline could finish, they were out the door and hoisting the stretcher into the ambulance. She knew it was her responsibility to call Leo's family and explain what had happened. She felt so guilty. What could she tell them? She called Leo's son, David, and his daughter, Melissa. She did not know how to get in touch with John, but she called the school to tell Alchemy the awful news. She knew Alchemy would know how to track down her father. When Madeline explained to Alchemy what had happened, Alchemy insisted on going with Madeline to the hospital. She gave the school permission to allow Alchemy to come to her grandfather's house.

"Wait for me, Maddy! I'm gonna go to the hospital with you!" Alchemy cried out in fear.

"I'll wait for you, Alchemy. Please, please drive carefully. He's going to be all right, Alchemy. I just know he is," Madeline prayed silently as she hung up the phone and waited for Alchemy to arrive. A half an hour later, Alchemy's car came careening down the lane to the front of the house. She jumped out of the car and ran into the house.

"Come on, let's go!" Alchemy demanded.

"Let me drive, Alchemy. You're too upset."

"I don't care who drives! Let's just get the hell out of here, Maddy!"

She started the car, and Alchemy jumped in the passenger seat. Just then, Madeline remembered the journal. She looked at Alchemy and said, "Hold on a minute. I forgot something." Madeline jumped out of the car and ran to the house.

"What are you doing?" Alchemy yelled

"I'll be right back!" Madeline responded.

By that time, Alchemy had become frustrated with Madeline. When Madeline came running back out with a book in her hand, Alchemy almost lost it.

"Grandpa's in the hospital, maybe dead, and you need reading material??!"

"Take it easy, Alchemy. I have so much to tell you, but let's get to the hospital first. Leo was unconscious, but he had a steady pulse. His will to live matches the will of this house. He'll make it, I promise."

Alchemy tapped her fingers against the window, and Madeline could see that she was really upset. She had never seen Alchemy cry, but she was dangerously close to it now.

"I promise, Alchemy. Leo's going to be OK." Alchemy stared for just an instant at Madeline, and then she turned her head and looked at the scenery flying by. She hoped she was right.

It had been almost three hours after Leo's fall when Madeline and Alchemy arrived at the hospital. The nurse at the front desk happily told Alchemy and Madeline that Leo had regained consciousness and that his children were already in the emergency area with him. At that time, no one else would be allowed to go back until the others came out. The nurse then directed them to the waiting room. Madeline winced when she sat down on the orange Formica chair, but she figured her discomfort was earned. She felt terrible about everything, and she felt responsible for Leo's fall. He had probably been coming to her room when he fell. She ventured a peek over at Alchemy sitting on another hard orange chair, who sat sullenly and fidgeted with her earrings. How would she ever explain herself to Alchemy? To Leo? As soon as Leo was well enough to talk, he'd want answers. And what would she tell him?

Alchemy couldn't sit still. She walked out of the waiting area, and Madeline watched as she paced back and forth, looking through the tiny emergency window, hoping to get a view of anyone coming to tell her about Leo. Madeline remembered the book in her hand. As she went to open it, an obviously very old piece of paper fell out. Out of curiosity, she began to read it:

∽

Dear Miss Adeline,

The doctor tells me I don't have much more time to live. I am writing to tell you of my undying love for you. Even though I am in so much pain, when you are with me, I am so happy that the pain seems to disappear. I want you to live a happy life."

The rest was a blur that Madeline couldn't decipher. It was signed by a man named *Jacob Mordecai Lee.*

🍁   🍁   🍁

Alchemy eventually made enough noise to the nurses to get her aunt and uncle out of the emergency area so Alchemy could see her Grandpa Leo. As they sat in the sterile waiting area, they made small talk with Madeline, but her mind was over a hundred years away with Adeline and Jacob Mordecai Lee. She just wanted to be alone so she could finish reading the journal. When Alchemy returned, she was so distracted by everything that had happened that when her aunt and uncle insisted that she go to dinner with them and spend the night, she made no protest. Madeline told Alchemy she would call in her absence to school for the following day. Madeline silently thanked them, and she declined their invitation to join them, telling them she wanted to get back to the house to make sure everything was secure. She really just wanted to be alone to think about what she needed to do. Instead of sleeping that night, as she intended, she read the journal from beginning to end. She had never cried so much in her life.

The whole journal immortalized the deep love Adeline had for Jacob Mordecai Lee and the deep love Adeline knew he had for her. Adeline related tales he told of his family, the battles he had fought, the demons he had banished, and how she knew she was the woman who had brought him back from the brink of death. Page after page of declarations to her beloved Mordy, and all for naught. He had vowed never to hurt her as the other men in her life had, but he had, unwillingly. He died…how Adeline must have suffered.

Madeline couldn't help but think about the similarities between herself and Adeline…they seemed like perfect silhouettes. The names…Maddy…Addie… both nurses…both suffering losses in love…both losing a parent…what did it all mean? The picture, so striking in its resemblance to her…she was beginning to feel a heavy sense of déja vu, but it was fleeting and frightening. She needed, no, she wanted answers. And the writing on the wall…what did it all mean?

CHAPTER 11

Cedarvine Convalescent Home, October 10, 1864

Adeline's Journal

    Jacob Mordecai Lee…without him my life would have no meaning. Life began for me the day I saw his face. There is no existence without him. This feeling…I promised myself I would never let this happen again. But his presence grips me body and soul. He is the light that I so crave. He gives me meaning, a reason to keep breathing…yet, I fear. The pain, the hurt, that comes with love; I couldn't bear it again. Roger, the first man I ever loved, made me feel so intensely joy and pain I would have never dreamt possible. I cannot explain the pain I experienced. Then William…I thought it was the last straw; he made me see that love is something I was not destined to have. But Mordy…I cannot imagine going on without him. There would be nothing worth living for. They say that everything happens for a reason. This war, all this death and suffering, it seems like no good can come from it. Jacob and Adeline. How did I let this happen to myself? I am in love again. I am no longer in control of my feelings. He occupies every second, every inch of my thoughts. I love him. I love him. What has happened to me? Whenever I'm around him I feel so elated, enraptured, intoxicated by his presence. Finally free after years of metaphorical entrapment. It feels just like falling. Oh, I hope I don't hit the ground this time.

    It is so endearing to see his dark eyes light up when I walk into a room, like a child who has just received an unexpected gift. His warm smile makes me melt every time, without fail. His dark hair is always disheveled; the tousled waves hang down over his tanned face. His appearance is a contradiction, his individual features are almost childlike, but his face as a whole gives off an air of masculinity and courage. It's in his eyes, the twinkle; it's like he knows something no one else does, a secret joke, or my thoughts. I can't help loving his quirks, like the way he gestures with his face to show his appreciation or delight. His charm has permeated my love-damaged heart. There's no turning back for me now. My love for him is so strong. If only he were well. I fear he will never be. It seems his injury has pained him forever; I cannot continue to watch him go on in this manner. I pray to God every night for his well-being and safekeeping. If I had one wish, I would wish for Mordy's recovery. His pain does not seem to bother him the way it bothers me. Sometimes I will see a moment of agony in his eyes, but he rarely complains, and he always displays such a cheery disposition outwardly. Oh, God, please let him live. I cannot imagine the pain he is feeling. Oh, Mordy, how I love you. I remain hopeful, as I am always looking for signs of recovery, though it may only be wishful thinking on my part. Some days he seems so well, so alive, and other days he doesn't have the strength to get out of bed. He just has to live. Without him I cannot go on. His spirited laugh assures me that everything will be fine.

Dr. Jennings is calling; I hope everyone is all right.

CHAPTER 12

Lebanon, Tennessee, May 2003

Madeline and Alchemy arrived at the hospital early in the afternoon. They'd both been anxious, especially after Alchemy returned home from the night spent at her aunt's house. After Leo's accident, the doctor had wanted to keep him overnight to run some tests and take some more x-rays. Now they were here again, waiting for the results.

The car ride over had been long and silent. Neither of them wanted to talk, satisfied to sit, each with her own thoughts. It was much the same way when they reached the hospital. It was visiting hours, so the lobby was crowded. Alchemy sat, staring at the uninteresting patterns on the floor while Madeline checked with information to see if Leo had been moved to another room since the day before. He was in the same place, the receptionist informed Madeline. Finally, they made their way down the long hall toward Leo's room. When they reached his room, the doctor was there, checking on Leo. The doctor greeted the somber pair warmly, and reassured them that the tests were all looking good, but that Leo would have to stay another day for observation. The scowl on Leo's face told both Madeline and Alchemy that Leo was feeling better. While Alchemy went and sat in the chair beside Leo's bed, the doctor talked with Madeline. After the doctor departed, Madeline went to the other side of the bed to talk to Leo. Madeline was just about to open her mouth to ask how Leo was feeling when she realized he had dozed off. Suddenly, her cell phone rang, and she quickly turned off the ringer. She excused herself and left the room so she wouldn't disturb Leo.

Even though Alchemy recognized Leo's mood and knew being told he must stay in the hospital another day was the cause of it, he looked more frail than she had ever seen him. Nothing like the stubborn old man she knew. It worried her that one day she would end up like that: mindful and full of memory but the inhabitant of a body that was slowly failing, like a rotting old home, like Grandpa's home, which you knew, one day, would finally give out. One day the load would be too heavy, and by internal or external force, it would collapse from the strain, the body taking the thought with it. And this is where it would end, for her, and for Grandpa Leo, here in a dreary hospital room like this one. Glancing around, she took in the room, imagining it like a coffin or an Egyptian tomb.

The room was so dull yet complex, filled with machines that droned in steady voices, beeping, humming, more alive than the person they were charged to watch over. Everything was meticulously clean, too, and white: the walls, the ceiling, the floor, everything. Even the few colors that existed in this doldrums were boring: a pale yellow for Leo's bed cover, the faded navy chair that Alchemy sat in with its small red diamond pattern. There was not a single thing in that room that might distract a person from thinking. Alchemy wondered how miserable it must be to have to sit in a room like this, miserable and with nothing to take your mind off it. A hospital should have colors, she decided, lots of colors. It should be like the room they take you to at the pediatrician's, the one with the bright vivid stripes on the walls, colorful cartoon animals everywhere, and, of course, a sweet lollipop at the end of it all.

These thoughts, and others, entered and left Alchemy's head as she waited quietly. She thought about Leo, and Madeline's vagueness about what had happened to him. Alchemy also thought about the house, about a TV show she'd seen, and any number of other irrelevant things. Eventually, she thought about where Madeline had gone. So, after asking the slumbering Leo's pardon, she got up in search of his caretaker.

Alchemy did not find her outside the door. The brightly lit hallway was empty, just a long, boxy white tunnel. Thinking that she might have gone down to the lobby, Alchemy started toward the elevator that would take her to the first floor. She passed the nurses' station. One was sitting at her desk, chatting in front of a glowing screen; another was leaning on the opposite side of the desk, talking to the first. Both were short, portly women with curly hair and toothpaste-colored uniforms. Alchemy ignored the disapproving looks they gave her and continued on down the hallway. As she rounded the corner to head for the elevator, she heard a voice up ahead. Recognizing it as Madeline's, Alchemy slowed down her walk.

Madeline was in an alcove, an inlet in the wall where the two bathroom doors faced each other with the water fountain between. She was talking to someone on her phone. The conversation was heated. Obviously, someone was yelling at Madeline. Alchemy couldn't understand the person's words, but they were loud enough that she could hear them. Madeline was struggling to keep her own tone even.

"Listen, this may take a little longer than we thought. There was an accident, and Leo's in the hospital. He'll be fine, and they're running some tests now. He's still not well, though...Ron, will you calm down. I told you, I'll get him to sign the papers, but it's just that...I know we don't have time, but I told you, the man's in the hospital, Ron. No. No, Ron, I'm not going to put this on him now...because he's injured! He's not well! And...I just don't think I can do this. Let me work with his children. They're more convinced now than ever that he needs to sell. What? You can't be serious. God, you can be so cold! I just don't...I don't care! I can get along without your 'advice'! Good-bye!"

The last words faded into the background as Alchemy hurried back around the corner and down the hall, back to the room before Madeline could realize she'd been spied on. Alchemy got back to the hospital room just as another intern arrived, a middle-aged man, in his late forties, with an already balding head of hair and a narrow face that seemed too thin. He was bent over a chart held in his hand, and when Alchemy entered, he said hello and asked if she was related to Leo. Alchemy gave him a distracted nod. He said that Leo checked out all right, nothing seriously damaged, but that he'd be feeling some discomfort for the next few days and should get a lot of rest. Alchemy wasn't really paying much attention. She wondered what it all meant. *Who was Ron, what papers was she talking about, and why was she talking to her boss that way about Grandpa Leo?*

CHAPTER 13

Cedarvine Convalescent Home, October 9, 1864

Mordecai awoke with a start. At once his fair lady was at his side, the beautiful maiden with flames cascading around her, a calm gaze staring him in the eyes. He met the caring look of affection with one of his own, the gentle nurse sitting on the edge of his white bed and caressing his brow with the back of one of her pale hands, as perfect as finely crafted porcelain. Mordecai grasped her delicate hand, saying gallantly to her, "Adeline, how your eyes quench the fires that rage in my heart and lay my fears to rest. My nightmares disappear when you touch me."

Adeline stifled a laugh as she took her hand back, gently patting him on the shoulder and whispering, "Hold on, love. Allow me to wipe the beads of sweat away before you profess your love to me…again."

Adeline stood from her position and hurried to a nearby cabinet containing medical bandages and wipes. She opened the door and collected several of the wipes before closing it back up, turning to find Mordecai sitting on the side of his bed. "Jacob Mordecai Lee, get yourself situated at once! You needn't be sitting up. Lie back down immediately before you faint."

The soldier gave her a disobedient wave of his hand before standing up and saying, "I'm a lieutenant, Madam." He reached for his boots. "I fear that I pull rank over your direct authority and shall decline accepting your order to—to—oh, dear."

Adeline could only watch in horror as Mordecai tipped over and fell to a heap in the floor. She was crouching beside his prone form in an instant. She had been flippantly replying with, "Women are always correct on such matters, sir. Take this fact to heart," but when he fell, the sarcasm gave way to fear.

"My dear, Adeline," Mordecai began as he was helped up by Adeline, "I take your every breath to heart. Your every breath gives me life." He winked, and in mock anger, Adeline sighed and tossed a wipe at him, which he managed to catch, bringing forth a grin to his serene features. He leaned against the bed.

As Adeline turned around she let loose a smile, saying, "If only everyone were as eloquent as you…"

"Well, then the world would be much more trite, I suppose. Then I would have to find a new way to differentiate myself from others. And I am sincerely lazy, so that would be an appalling thing."

She shrugged off the hands that suddenly rested upon her shoulders, and striding to the door said, "Well, if you're going to continue to have nightmares, you really should share your complaints and fears and the like with Phillip. He would be honored to listen to them, so feel free to pay him a visit today. I'm sure he'll make all the pains of the past go away."

"Surely you're not leaving me, Addie…this is a crucial moment in…well, I don't know, but where are you off to so soon?" Mordecai gave her a pleading gaze.

"Puppy-dog eyes won't work on me, Lieutenant," Adeline said with a dismissive gesture.

"But…but Dr. Jennings frightens me…how can he help?"

Adeline paused. "Come now, Phillip is harmless."

Mordecai laughed once before grinning. "It's the needles I'm frightened of, ma'am."

"You're hopeless," Adeline said, rolling her eyes and opening the door. As she was about to head through the frame, Mordecai cleared his throat. Adeline didn't even turn. "Yes?"

"Can I have a glass of water?"

"Certainly, it's in the pantry, love." She discerned the sigh from behind her, so she turned and strode back to Mordecai. "How about I play you a song upon the piano later today? It always cheers you up. Or would you rather the kind Doctor give you some medicine…he has plenty of needles that are in need of patients."

Mordecai tilted his head, resting a hand under his chin and pondering the situation. "Well, let me consider...sharp needles or a sharp tongue. What's choice number three?"

"Go to sleep and have more nightmares," Adeline said, the sunlight streaming in through the window illuminating her brilliant white dress and scarlet hair.

"Well, in that case I'll certainly come out to the piano to hear you make music that is sweet and melodic to my ears," Mordecai said, taking one of Adeline's hands in his and planting a gentle kiss upon the warm flesh.

"Excellent," she said, letting her hand fall back to her side. "I'll see you later then. Think of a song you'd like me to play, but in the meantime, Phillip is in his office upstairs. Talk to him about your nightmares. I'm sure he can help. And try not to get into any trouble." With that she was gone, the door once more closed.

Mordecai sat down upon the edge of his bed, looking at the blank door. "Oh yes, Adeline, I shall...*try*. If I miserably fail, that's another thing entirely. See Dr. Jennings, you say? Well, I heartily shall disagree. Crazy old coot probably lives for the satisfaction of plunging syringes deep into unsuspecting patients' veins and twisting the needle violently and painfully...oh yes, indeed...wait, why am I talking to myself? I need to get some fresh air."

Mordecai stood and went to his window, unlocked it, and pulled the smooth glass upward so that he could take a moment and feel the cool breeze. From his position he leaned forward, resting his arms on the windowpane and let the wind toss his hair. The chill October breeze caressed the rugged stubble attempting to grow upon his normally clean-shaven features, forcing a smile out of him. "What a day this shall be."

Mordecai eased his way back inside his room, letting the window close with a gentle *thud*. He crept to the door, slowly turning the doorknob so as not to disturb anyone. As he left his room with silent footsteps, he saw Dr. Jennings' helper, Nicholas, standing directly in front of him, staring at him strangely. The lad started toward him. "Sir, are you supposed to be walking around in your condition?"

Mordecai shrugged lightly. "What condition? I feel perfectly fine, Nicholas." As he began to walk past the lad, the young man stood in his way. "Yes?"

"Are you sure? You look pretty bad," the lad said, arching a brow questioningly.

"This is the way I always look; are you insulting me now?"

"Of course not, sir, I meant no harm…I just thought you looked sickly," the lad stated in his defense.

"Well, those lacking the proper knowledge should not acknowledge knowledge," Mordecai said staggering away from the lad.

Nicholas stopped him once again. "That's heaps of knowledge, if you don't mind me saying so, sir."

"Of course not," Mordecai said. He actually thought the lad was a good thinker, very mature for his age. He had seen the lad, but had never previously engaged in conversation.

Mordecai put his hand upon Nicholas' shoulder, looking him straight in the eye, saying gently to him. "Well, Nicholas, would you kindly move aside?"

"It depends."

"Upon what?" Mordecai sighed.

"Upon what you have to offer me as compensation for me keeping my mouth shut." Nicholas stood firmly in place, not budging an inch.

Mordecai thought for a moment before calmly stating: "I can only offer friendship, my young friend."

Nicholas chuckled once before replying, "Whatever that's worth. I was thinking along the lines of coins."

Mordecai frowned. "How about if I let you take a venture out the closest window?"

Nicholas' eyes widened in surprise as he nodded curtly, whispering: "S-sure, your wish is my command…sir." At once the lad moved aside, allowing Mordecai to pass by, though as Mordecai prepared to head upstairs, he turned to face him once more.

As Nicholas was about to enter a doorway at the end of the corridor, Mordecai called out, "And, young Nicholas, one more thing."

"Yes?" the boy inquired, pausing, his hand upon the doorknob.

"Where might I find some parchment and a quill, Nicholas?"

The boy pondered momentarily before saying, "The good doctor would have those materials, I believe."

"Are you certain?" Mordecai called out, dreading his visit to Dr. Jennings.

"Yes, sir, I certainly am."

Mordecai walked over to the boy, wincing in pain as he tried to crouch before Nicholas. Finally, he just remained standing, caressing the area around his wound. "Could you direct me to it? I really do not feel like going alone to see Dr. Jennings."

Nicholas smiled mischievously. "Well, fine. I'll take you up there, sir."

Nicholas led him to the stairs, then went up slowly and waited for Mordecai at the top of the steps. It took Mordecai a long time, but Nicholas ushered him to a door at the end of the hallway, and then opened the door and urged the soldier inside. Mordecai nodded his head in thanks to the boy's aid. He walked in, hearing the boy close the door, whispering, "I'll come back later for my *coins*, my new friend. Farewell."

Mordecai smiled at the lad before the door closed. He twisted around to the man sitting behind the desk. "Dr. Jennings, you're not too busy to see me?"

The older man started. "Not at all. You may call me Phillip, Jacob, as always."

Mordecai frowned. "Certainly, Dr. Jennings, and you may call me Lieutenant Lee, as always."

"Ah, you have a healthy respect for your beloved army status, I see, Jacob," Dr. Jennings replied with a crooked smile.

"Dr. Jennings—"

"—Phillip, Jacob—"

"—Lieutenant Lee, Dr. Jennings—"

"Fine, Jacob, have it your own way. Call me Phillip when you're ready."

Mordecai grinned and said, "Why certainly, Phill—I mean…well, have it your own way. Phillip."

"Now, Jacob, what was it you wanted to talk to me about?" Dr. Jennings leaned across the desk, gesturing toward a chair.

Mordecai remained standing. "Who said anything about talking? I certainly didn't."

"Oh, yes, stubborn as usual; a certain nurse told me of nightmares you've been having…"

Mordecai rolled his eyes as he took a seat. "Ten guesses who that could have been," he whispered under his breath.

Dr. Jennings smiled as he said, "Well, considering we only have two nurses on duty, I should hope you are well enough to get it correct at least once with those ten guesses, Jacob."

"I didn't come here to be mocked," Mordecai said with a flash of hostility clouding his gaze.

"And mocked you shall not be. So, tell me, why do you imagine you are having these nightmares?" Dr. Jennings opened a drawer and took out a quill, ink, and some sheets of parchment.

"We get together and all you can think of is recording the level of my sanity," Mordecai said with a laugh. "Wonderful."

"Indeed. Now, proceed, if you will, with the answer to the question."

"Very well, but I can assure you I am not insane, and if you even consider that I am, I'll find my saber and poke you like you do your patients with needles…"

"Of course, though I must note the fact you are avoiding the question." Dr. Jennings wrote several things upon the paper after dipping the quill in the dark ink. Mordecai leaned forward to see what the doctor was writing, but as he did Dr. Jennings stopped and smiled. "Confidential, of course." He covered the notes with his arm.

"Fancy that. They're my own thoughts, and they're confidential to me…" Mordecai let his hands rest upon his knees as he slouched forward. "Well, if you insist upon knowing, then I'll tell you."

"Ah, progress at last!" Dr. Jennings said with a grin.

Mordecai lowered his eyes and whispered something under his breath. "*Death.*"

Dr. Jennings stopped recording and let his eyes meet with Mordecai's. "What do you mean?"

"Doctor…it was all around me. This black plague…it swallowed up many good friends of mine and…it keeps haunting my dreams, preventing me from having a good night's rest."

"Ah, yes, war seems to do that, it appears. Go on."

"I keep reliving the battle that happened, as if it was completely my fault and now God has decided to torment me for all eternity. I can't live like this. When will these specters of the past leave my troubled heart alone?" Mordecai shivered at the thought of having another one of the nightmares he had grown so accustomed to reliving.

Dr. Jennings paused after writing down several notes and then looked up. "I'm truly sorry, Jacob. It appears that nervous hands beget a nervous mind. In this situation, your body has had so much trauma from the wound in battle, that you feel the need to cause additional pain from a mental standpoint, it appears. I can give you medicine for pain and apply salves to injuries, but what can one truly do for emotional distress?"

Mordecai let his head tilt forward sadly. "It appears that death will be my only salvation. Is that all my future holds?"

Dr. Jennings sighed, dropping the quill. "No one can prolong the inevitable, Jacob. We all die one day, and if God is with you, why should you fear death? Do not sulk so much, cheer up; the fact that you're alive now is what matters."

Mordecai cleared his throat before asking, "Oh, and doctor…would you care to lend me some parchment and something with which to write? I've used up my supply of parchment, and I've filled every page of the journals I had with me."

Dr. Jennings held Mordecai's gaze before shrugging lightly. "Of course, no harm could come of it, unless you are so distressed by nightmares you intend to impale yourself using this pen I shall give you…"

With a smile, Mordecai waited as Dr. Jennings retrieved parchment, ink and a quill pen from his desk.

"Oh, yes, are you feeling any better, Jacob?"

Mordecai frowned as he replied, "Well, my wound seems mostly healed. What torment is there left to put me through? Wait…is there a needle involved?"

"No, Jacob, I was just wondering…" Dr. Jennings said, drawing the sentence out, leaving Mordecai with the thought that there was more than met the eye to this sensitive subject.

"Is there anything I need to know?"

Dr. Jennings smiled as he shook his head rapidly, "No, no, my boy, nothing to fret about; just curious if you were feeling well, which, if I judged by the excessive amounts of sarcasm which you have delivered at this meeting, I should say you are at tip-top shape. Here are your items." He held his hand out, the paper, ink bottle, and pen resting on his palm.

Mordecai shrugged casually as he accepted the offered supplies, pocketed them, said his thanks, and left promptly, rolling his eyes as he went his way. Dr. Jennings called out, "And close the door, please, if you would. If you happen upon Nicholas, send him to me."

And with that final note, Mordecai closed the door.

"Now for the grand finale," Mordecai said to himself as he strode down the hall. From the dark confines of a doorway, he saw Nicholas peeking out at him. "Nicholas, Dr. Jennings wishes to see you now. Feel free to show yourself at any time." As Nicholas passed him, he tossed a coin in the air which the keen-eyed Nicholas scooped before it hit the floor.

"Thanks, sir," Nicholas said as he walked toward Dr. Jennings' office.

He stared at the winding stairs leading to the first floor. He cautiously went over the thoughts in his mind. *Okay, Mordy, you can do this. You're a lieutenant. You've won battles, commanded hundreds of soldiers, and you're afraid to walk down a staircase without aid?*

Taking a careful step and letting his foot rest upon the wood, Mordecai took the railing tightly in his hands, continuing down the stairs at a slow pace, hands shaking. If his side reacted to such sudden movements down the stairs, he risked tumbling to a painful landing. After a few moments he stepped upon the first floor, pleased with himself.

Silently congratulating himself upon his achievement, Mordecai glanced around to make sure no one was nearby. He heard several voices speaking in a room close by, but that was all. He hastily fumbled around in his pocket, pulling out the writing accoutrements. The wrinkled sheet was disgraceful for what he planned on using it for, but it was all he had.

The pen was in his hand before he knew it, and the ink stand he placed on the wood which covered the piano keys. Taking a seat upon the bench before the piano that rested beneath the stairs, Mordecai took a deep breath. He placed the paper on the piano top, and then tried his best to scribble several words.

ॐ

Dear Adeline, I have adored you from the very first day your smiling face greeted me. I could not imagine spending the rest of my life alone, without you...everything and everyone I used to know is gone. You are all that I have left, but you fulfill my every need and desire. Adeline, my heart, my beautiful dreamer, will you marry me?

Mordy

After finishing the note, Mordecai let the ink dry and rolled the parchment to the thickness of a ring finger. He put the ink bottle back in his pocket, and though he hated to use his fresh handkerchief to wrap the quill in, he did and pocketed it along with the ink bottle. He smiled warmly as he reached a hand down into another pocket, retrieving his most prized possession: the ring from the family of his third cousin, General Robert E. Lee. The ring had been passed down through many members of the Lee family, and his mother had given it to him to present to the woman he would wed. The cherished possession was slipped around the parchment like a groom would slip the ring on his beloved's finger.

His first thought was to place the ring inside the piano and hope that during one of their "concerts," Adeline would hit a flat note and feel compelled to discover the source of the problem. The piano top was heavy, and he worried about countless other things that might go wrong with the plan. Any other hiding places he thought about brought another round of doubts. He knew he had to hurry, as anyone could come down the stairs or through the house at any minute. He heard Adeline in the kitchen, and it sounded as though her footsteps were coming closer to the door which divided the kitchen from the foyer. His sweaty hands rubbed the brocaded cover of the piano bench. The bench…that was it! The bench! He stood up, opened the lid, and thanked his lucky stars for the idea. Then he picked up the *Stephen Foster Songbook* which had come to mean so much to him and Adeline over the last months. He opened the book to the page with the song "Beautiful Dreamer"…he thought of it as their song, and he gently placed the parchment proposal and ring between the pages. The bulge in the book was obvious.

Just then he heard the kitchen door start to swing open. He stashed the songbook underneath other sheet music. The lid went down with a THUD just as Adeline entered the foyer.

As Mordecai prepared to turn around and head back to his room, he heard a sigh from behind him. Twisting around, he noticed Adeline tapping a foot and giving him a playful look. "Mordy, what sort of trouble are you getting into?"

"What? Whatever do you mean? Why would you instantly consider that I was doing something wrong?" Mordecai attempted to look as innocent as possible but his flushed face made Adeline pause.

"I was close by and I heard a noise, so I came in here. I was just in the pantry, fixing some food for you, ravenous animal that you are," Adeline said with a mischievous grin.

"Did you now? Must have been a rat or something of the likes. I heard nothing." Mordecai raised a hand and let it run through his ragged hair, turning around uncomfortably and hoping she did not suspect anything was amiss.

Adeline lightly laughed and dismissed the subject. "Improbable, but not impossible, I suppose. Very well, what are you doing here? Did you see Phillip? Shouldn't you rest? Were you on your way to your room?"

"Just happened to be in the neighborhood. Thought I'd drop by the pantry and pay a visit to the food reserves," Mordecai said, facing her once more. She rolled her eyes and motioned for him to join her.

"I've made you a sandwich—"

"Getting fancy, aren't we?"

"—but if you get smart with me once more, I'll let Dr. Jennings feast upon it."

At this Mordecai silenced himself. "Such a dismal thought. Lead on, fair lady. You are the flame that lights my path, my *beautiful dreamer.*"

She shyly turned at the words and the tone of the words. She smiled, took his hand, and led him to the kitchen door. They walked slowly into the kitchen area, where two plates rested, sandwiches on both of them.

Mordecai gasped, "What a feast! Thank you kindly, dear Adeline. Whatever shall I do for such kindness shown to me by one of such a kind heart?" A strange look crossed Mordecai's face as he finished his comment. He swayed a bit in his chair.

Adeline paused, considering. "Perhaps we'll think of something…later you can sweep the floors. How does that sound?"

Mordecai grasped his side, a grimace crossing his features.

Adeline sighed. "Oh, come now, Mordy, you're being childish…" Adeline's heart froze over as she saw a tear forming at the corner of Mordecai's eye. With a quivering voice, Adeline managed to whisper: "Mordy?"

With a lurch, Mordecai tumbled to the side, sprawling on the floor as his chair went sliding from beneath him. Adeline's sight was suddenly obscured as tears began to form, her own chair sent airborne as she threw herself out of it and onto the floor in a heap beside Mordecai.

"Mordy!" She stroked his forehead, which had sweat accumulating rapidly. She shouted for Dr. Jennings and Rebecca. Adeline cradled Mordecai's head in her lap, resting her head upon his.

"Do not fear, love, everything is going to be all right…can you hear me? I just want you to know that I love you with all my heart, though I may not show it as much as I truly desire." A solitary tear fell from her moist eyes as footfalls were heard on the stairs. Dr. Jennings' voice called out inquiring what was wrong. Adeline's vision blurred once more…then she suddenly felt faint.

The last thing she saw was Dr. Jennings pulling her to the side and laying something soft under her head…then there was only darkness…and thoughts of Mordecai…

CHAPTER 14

Cedarvine Manor, May 2003

After having come back from the hospital, Alchemy sat in the living room with Madeline. Madeline was in deep thought as she stared out of the window. Alchemy began to think about the phone call that she had overheard a couple of hours previously. *Should I ask Madeline about all this talk? Maybe it's just a big misunderstanding.* Alchemy couldn't sit in the same room with Madeline; she was being too quiet for the young teenager. Alchemy stood up and began walking towards the kitchen.

"Madeline, I'm going to make some lemonade. All this quietness and thinking is making me thirsty. Would you like some?"

Madeline looked up from her deep thoughts as though she hadn't heard a word Alchemy said.

"What? Lemonade? Sure." Madeline was distracted by something and went back to looking out the window, fading back into her deep thoughts.

What on earth is she thinking about? Besides, Leo isn't home yet, so any papers she has to get him to sign, she has to do it when Leo is here, but what papers does she need to get signed? Alchemy stirred the packet of powder and water together as she tried to think through what she had overheard. Moments later, Alchemy walked back out into the living room where Madeline was still in the same position looking out the window. Setting the pitcher down on the stand next to the crystal glasses, she began to pour herself some lemonade and then looked at Madeline. Madeline sat, looking very nervous and upset at the same time.

"Madeline, you don't look so good. Are you feeling okay?"

"Yeah, I'm okay, I'm just really exhausted. With Leo's fall, going back and forth to the hospital, and not getting any sleep, it's wearing me out." Her eyes looked as though something haunted their depths, and she sighed tiredly.

"I'm going back to the hospital this evening to check on Grandpa Leo. I want to see if he's really feeling better, and besides, it's so boring in those hospital rooms, he probably would like someone else besides my badgering Aunt Melissa and Uncle David to keep him company," Alchemy said, taking a sip of the lemonade. Alchemy had waited long enough. She charged right in to what had been bothering her.

"Madeline, I heard you talking to someone on the phone, back at the hospital. You said something about getting my grandpa to sign off the papers. What were you talking about? What papers? And who is Ron?"

Madeline looked up at Alchemy, shocked by the confrontation. At the same time, she began searching for words.

"Alchemy, the papers…uh, the papers are for my boss, Ron. I had told him about Leo's accident, and he wanted me to get Leo to sign the papers to let him know that everything that has happened at the hospital, and that all the medication he has taken is correct, and that we wouldn't be held responsible…" Madeline lied, looking away quickly and taking a sip of lemonade.

Alchemy began to think to herself as she looked at the broken look on Madeline's face.

"Since Ron is a doctor, why didn't he come to the hospital to see Leo?"

There was no reply from Madeline.

"Madeline, please talk to me. I need to understand."

Madeline rose, and started slowly walking out of the room. Alchemy followed. Madeline moved up the stairs, and Alchemy thought she might be heading for her room, but Madeline passed her bedroom door. She seemed intent on studying the pictures on the wall. As Madeline walked down the hall, she kept stopping at different pictures on the walls, seemingly looking for answers to the questions she knew Alchemy had. Alchemy sensed Madeline's need to skirt whatever was bothering her, so she decided she would play along…for a while. So, as they stopped to look at the various pictures on the wall, Alchemy explained that many of them were family members from previous owners of the house. Then they stopped at the last picture. It was a picture of Adeline, the same nurse she had seen in the picture with the soldier in the wheelchair.

"I don't care what you say. Adeline looks just like you, Maddy. You can't deny it. It's too obvious."

"Yeah, I guess you're right." Madeline laughed hollowly, but the pained expression on her face remained.

Across the hall on the wall next to Leo's storage room, in a brown wooden picture frame, the face of an elderly woman sitting in a dark wooden chair gazed toward the pictures on the opposite wall.

"And who is this?" Madeline asked.

"That...I think that is Rebecca, the other nurse at the infirmary," Alchemy replied looking at the woman. Alchemy and Madeline moved to the room next to the picture. The walls had been painted a bright yellow at one time, and though the paint was cracking, the room still looked very inviting.

"If I lived in this house, this would be my room," stated Madeline.

"I know, I like this room, too," Alchemy said looking around the room at all the old belongings.

Over by the window, on top of the windowsill, sat five pairs of shoes; four pairs of the shoes were wooden and the other pair was leather. Madeline walked over to a pair and picked them up and put them on. They were a wooden, light brown pair, and they had a point at the tip of the shoe, which made them look like an elf's shoes. Madeline then looked at Alchemy and finally smiled. The shoes were very comfortable, and Alchemy knew why Madeline was smiling. Alchemy had once put on the shoes, and she thought the very same thing. They were the most comfortable shoes she had ever worn.

"I didn't think they would be comfortable at all, since they're wooden," said Madeline. This small thing finally broke the ice between Madeline and Alchemy. They were so wrapped up in the wonder of the house that Alchemy forgot her suspicions, and Madeline deliberately let her predicament slide to the back burner of her mind.

"Let me show you something else, Maddy," Alchemy urged Madeline out of the room and down the hall. The room they went into was an exceptionally dirty room. There was dust everywhere. It had big brown packing boxes scattered throughout the room. Many of the boxes contained pictures and journals and hospital documents. Other boxes contained very old items, which Madeline thought must have been very cherished items from people in the past. The pictures were covered in dust. Madeline wiped off one of the pictures with her shirtsleeve, and she saw an elderly man. He was tall and thin with grey hair. He was sitting in an office chair looking out of the window.

"Who is this?" Madeline asked examining it closely.

"That is Dr. Jennings. He was really into his work and what he did," Alchemy replied. "Remember, we talked about him when you first got here…you said that was your dad's name, too?"

Thinking of her father made Madeline uncomfortable, so to change the subject she said, "Oh, I didn't realize there was so much history in this house. I can see why you and your grandfather love this house so much." Madeline's eyes began to fill up with tears.

"Madeline, are you all right? What's the matter?" Alchemy asked.

"Oh, it's nothing. I'm sorry I'm acting like this. I'm just having a hard time with all of this. This house has so much history, and it's so very important and…"

"S-h-h…calm down. It's going to be okay," Alchemy broke in.

Just then, Madeline spotted a brown, leather-covered journal with a heart carved in the middle of it. She pulled it out from between two other books. "Do you mind if I read it?" asked Madeline.

"I've never seen that one before. I've found some and read them, but that one looks different. Sure, you can look at it. I don't think the people from the past would care if you looked at it," Alchemy joked.

"I guess you're right," Madeline smiled as she opened the journal.

On the first page, the name Jacob M. Lee was inscribed. She flipped through a couple of pages, and all the pages had a little title, underlined, and a brief writing of that topic. Although the handwriting of the 1860s was hard to decipher, Madeline could see the meaning was clear and precise through most of the entries. Entries described people, places in and around the convalescent home, menus, and even musical notes that might have been penned to write a tune. She stopped when she came to the entry titled "Nurse Adeline."

∾

Nurse Adeline

I'm at the infirmary. My nurse is Adeline, and she is very nice. She showers me with special attention. Just the other day, she took me on a remarkable tour of the house and the garden, and then she became quite upset when I asked her about a room I had only heard about but never seen. It was the room with the writing on the wall. She begged for me never to leave my name there, and I solemnly promised Miss Adeline that she would never see my name on the wall. I've fallen in love, and rather quickly, with Miss Adeline. I'm not sure what I should *do. Whatever happens, I will never forget Miss Adeline, my beautiful dreamer. She will be in my heart <u>always</u>.*

Jacob M. Lee

Madeline put down the journal and looked at Alchemy. "Didn't you say you had read one of his journals? I can hear the passion in his words…this is just too much emotion for me."

She began to tear up, thinking about the situation she was in and feeling guilt for what she was doing. She slowly walked from the room and headed for the stairs. Alchemy picked up the discarded journal and followed Madeline down the stairs to the foyer where Madeline stopped beside the piano. Madeline sat down on the worn material of the old piano bench, smoothed by years of use. She began poking at the keys.

Both lost in their thoughts, Alchemy drifted toward the door saying, "Madeline, I think I'm going to go now and check on Grandpa Leo." Alchemy grabbed her keys and headed toward the door. She didn't see the tears slowly falling down Madeline's face.

CHAPTER 15

Cedarvine Convalescent Home, October 11, 1864

"Doctor, are you quite sure?" Rebecca's weathered face was wrinkled in concern.

"Absolutely. We both know how emotional Adeline can get, especially when it comes to these silly…infatuations of hers! I know they're not silly to dear Adeline, but I feel we must protect her in any way we can." Dr. Jennings took a deep breath, expelling the worry he felt.

"No. We can't have Adeline know of this. You will handle all shifts involving Mr. Lee until further notice. Not a word to Adeline, do you understand?" With a keen eye, Jennings watched her face for any sign of her intentions. She earnestly nodded her agreement, though inside she wondered how she could keep Adeline away from the sickroom.

"Excellent. You understand how much I appreciate your cooperation. You always have been a very capable nurse. We know how these things need to be done."

Rebecca wasn't entirely sure of that. Somehow, Adeline deserved to know, but Rebecca knew all too well what would happen if Adeline allowed her mixed-up emotions to get involved. Adeline could neglect her duties and might even end up disobeying Dr. Jennings just to get her way. No, this was for the best. In the end, Dr. Jennings was right.

"Sir, what's his condition? I need to know what signs to watch for," Rebecca asked.

"As far as I can tell, Mr. Lee's problem is…dangerous, to say the very least. I'm afraid his infection has returned." Rebecca gasped. Phillip nodded his somber agreement, then went on.

"I can't say it comes as a surprise really. He's been far too active as of late," he sighed as he clasped his hands behind his back. "That's why I had him brought up here, so I can be close by if he takes a turn for the worse. Infection at this point could mean certain death, and with Adeline's obvious feelings…"

Rebecca put a comforting hand on his shoulder. "Dr. Jennings, don't worry. She's a strong woman. She has gotten through tough times before, and so she shall once more."

"I agree…but still…" Dr. Jennings let the sentence fade, but Rebecca understood completely.

"We'll be there to help her through whatever happens. Have no fear," Rebecca calmly replied.

"Of course, you're right…as usual. I wonder how Mr. Lee is holding up as we speak?"

Rebecca shook her head sadly, dropping her hand from his shoulder. "I'll go check. Just have faith, Phillip. Pray for everyone this night; we all could use a blessing from God."

"That I can do, Rebecca," Phillip said with a haunted look upon his features. As Rebecca left his office, he took a seat behind his desk, exhausted. As he began praying silently, the exhaustion overtook him. His head fell forward on his chest, and the light snoring was joined by the low moans of the man who now resided in the room with the writing on the wall.

Mordecai let his head lull to the side, looking at the dust resting upon the railing of the bed. Expelling a gentle breath, he sent the dust careening away. He closed his eyes and let the pain slowly fade away. Every movement sent jolts of shocking pain discharging through his entire body. Mordecai had no idea what he had experienced, or why he was here, in this bed. Opening his eyes, he noticed a lone chair, the upholstery worn, like it had been used often. It looked familiar, but through the haze of fever, he couldn't grasp where he had seen it before. As he looked to his left, he saw the writing on the wall, but even that didn't send any alarms ringing through his feverished head.

Glancing around, he noticed familiar silhouettes in the darkness, haunting his vision. Gasping, he saw old comrades surrounding him, staring down upon his prone form. "Lt. Lee, finally you're seein' the truth for what it really is."

Mordecai gasped as Charlie Broodings took a step toward him, a ghastly hand nearing him. Mordecai shrunk back against the bed as he stammered, "W-what do you want from me?"

Charlie smiled as he shook his head sadly, then turned his gaze directly upon Mordecai. "You."

Eyes widening, Mordecai could do nothing as the ghosts that plagued his mind continued to come close to him, reaching for him. Their features were mutated, decayed from their previous state.

"Go away; I have no quarrel with you fiends!" Mordecai waved his arms at them weakly, a useless gesture.

At this Charlie laughed, stopping. "I would guess not, considerin' we are dead, my old friend. Thanks to you. All thanks to you, Lieutenant..."

The ghosts all started to reach for Mordecai when the sound of someone clearing his throat behind them stopped their hands. The spirits parted slowly, allowing Mordecai to see Maxwell standing before him. The old soldier threw his arms wide, the spirits on both sides of Mordecai disappearing instantly without any warning whatsoever. Maxwell glowed radiantly, saying to Mordecai, "Soon, my friend. Soon."

With a flash of light Maxwell was gone, and Mordecai was sitting up in his bed, wondering if that had really been a dream or if it was reality. His head fell against his pillow, a sigh coming forth from him. His eyes slowly registered the light coating of dust collected upon the railing of his bed. A dream...just a dream...

He did not know if he would be awake when Adeline came in to check on him, to find out what had gone wrong. Somehow he would have to tell her how much he loved her because his marriage proposal was so close at hand. He could no longer wait. Mordecai suddenly remembered the pen he had pocketed after writing the note that he had placed in the piano. With a faint smile at the fond memory, he feebly pulled the writing instrument out of his pocket.

With a final vestige of strength, Mordecai managed a horrible scribble:

Addie, I love you, my beautiful dreamer

—Mordy

His energy spent, the pen fell from his fingers. The last thing he heard was the utensil striking the hard floor. Mordecai let himself enter into a peaceful slumber, letting the sounds of the world fade away...

CHAPTER 16

❀

Cedarvine Manor, May 2003

Madeline's head was spinning; the long talk she had hoped to have with Alchemy hadn't materialized, and all the jumbled thoughts of her deception had left her feeling dizzy and unable to walk. Thinking of every lie she said spoken made her hate herself even more. *What am I doing?* Madeline searched her head for answers. There were none. She spun around on the piano bench and faced the piano once more as she reflected on the events of the last couple of weeks. Now that Alchemy had gone back to the hospital to check on Leo, Madeline had a little time to be by herself. Solitude and quiet: these were the two key ingredients to fixing a problem.

It had all started with Ron and his "chance of a lifetime." Ron, the most despicable man on the face of the earth. But if he was the most despicable man, what did that make her? She, Madeline Hightower, wasn't any better. She came into the home of a loving old man and tried to snatch it right out from under his feet. Leo had been kind and generous to her; he had been more of a father to her than her own had been.

"A-h-h," Madeline groaned when she reminded herself. "I've messed up, it's plain and simple. I can't erase the past and I can't start over again. So what do I do? I can try to fix my mistake. That's the only thing I can do." Madeline thought long and hard, once again searching for an answer that wasn't there. She closed her eyes and concentrated.

She slowly opened her eyes and looked down at the old ivory keys. She remembered Leo telling her that no one played it but that he would love to hear her play sometime. "Well, then, Leo, this one's for you," said Madeline aloud to the empty house.

She reached out her arms and stretched her fingers. They fell into place on the old, yellowed keys of the piano. Madeline breathed in deeply. It had been so long since she had played, but it was always relaxing for her. The song came into her mind immediately. It was her mother's favorite piece when she was still alive. *Nocturne in C Minor*. She began to play, and that old wonderful feeling took her in. Completely lost in the moment, Madeline didn't know anything except the piano. Everything that had happened that day was swept away with the soothing melodies of Chopin.

As the notes drifted away, she felt the need to play more, but her mind seemed to suddenly be blank. She wondered if the piano bench might yield some sheet music. She remembered the organized manner of her mother's music in the piano bench she sat on as a child. She stood up, lifted the cover to the screechy sounds of metal bearings rubbing years of misuse together, and gasped at the obviously old sheet music contained within the bench. She gingerly gathered up a pile of antiquated sheet music. Delighted by the find, she starting sorting through it and noticed a rather thick book-like collection. It seemed lumpy, and she worried whether she might come across some dead rodent or some other equally surprising find. Slowly opening the very old *Stephen Foster Songbook*, she discovered much more than a dead mouse. Inside, on the page of music titled "Beautiful Dreamer," in plain view, was an old piece of parchment rolled up with a ring around it to keep it in place. Madeline, in wonder, pulled the ring off of the rolled parchment. The ring, a beautiful ring, had a gold band with a good-sized diamond set in the middle accompanied by sapphires on either side of the diamond. She took the note, carefully opened it, and began reading.

❧

Dear Adeline, I have adored you from the very first day your smiling face greeted me. I could not imagine spending the rest of my life alone, without you...everything and everyone I used to know is gone. You are all that I have left, but you fulfill my every need and desire. Adeline, my heart, my beautiful dreamer, will you marry me?

Mordy

Madeline stared in disbelief. *Mordy? Adeline, will you marry me?* Adeline was beginning to become quite a fixture in the household. Mordy had to be the same Jacob Mordecai "Mordy" Lee mentioned in Adeline's journal. The note looked like it had been there for a very long time. Why would someone just leave it here? Did these two people break up and Mordy change his mind about proposing? Whatever became of these two? She was completely confused. This house, everything about it, was so secretive. Could she unravel its mystery? Madeline concentrated on everything: the note, the journal, all the pictures in the house. Wait! The pictures! Madeline, ring and note in hand, ran up the stairs to her room. She couldn't contain her excitement. Her heart was beating faster, and every step felt like a mile.

Up the steps she raced to her bedroom. Finally reaching the door, she swung it open and rushed to the bureau. There it was. The picture that had caught Madeline and drawn her in, ever since the first day that she had arrived. It was a simple picture of a woman in a nurse's uniform sitting with a man on a porch swing, but it might also be so much more. She took out the back of the picture frame and looked. Just as she had suspected, inscribed on the back of the picture in scrawling handwriting were two names: Adeline *Hightower* and Jacob Mordecai Lee with the date September 16, 1864.

"HIGHTOWER????? *Adeline Hightower?*" This was almost too much to take for Madeline. Her life up to this point had been like a carnival rollercoaster at times, but these last months seemed like the monster of the midway ride. She wanted off! Yet, the always-calm Madeline Hightower took a deep breath and thought about all she had discovered.

"This is amazing," Madeline said to herself, "This is truly amazing!" She had become so entwined in the mystery of the house, and now finding her name associated with the picture of the nurse who looked so much like her…and Adeline/Madeline as "nurses," both being hurt by men they thought they loved, and now finding the proposal and ring? This house was so much more than an old home in the path of a major road construction project. This house was full of history, *her history perhaps*, and Madeline had never even realized it. This could be the answer! Madeline thought. This might be how they could save the house!

The door opened downstairs.

"Madeline?" Alchemy called out. "Madeline, are you here?"

"I'm upstairs, Alchemy, in my room. Will you come here? I need to show you something."

Madeline heard the rush of feet coming up the stairs. She knew what she had to do. This charade couldn't go on any longer, even if it meant making Alchemy, Leo, and everyone else mad at her. The anger they would inevitably have toward her would be better than to continue living a lie.

"What's going on?" asked Alchemy.

"Oh, Alchemy!" Madeline realized she was letting her emotions take control, and she didn't even care anymore. "There's something I need to tell you, and it's not very easy for me." Alchemy stared at Madeline, confused.

"I'm not a nurse. I never even finished nursing school. I work with the Tennessee Roadway Engineering Company, and I was sent here to try to persuade your grandfather to sell his home. You must think I'm a terrible person."

Alchemy's face was a flaming red color at this point, which made Madeline's stomach turn. The seventeen year-old girl stood there quietly, not saying a word. Madeline sensed that Alchemy was trying as hard as she could to keep herself from throwing her fists up and screaming at Madeline.

"I wish you would say something, anything!" pleaded the helpless Madeline.

"Say something?" Alchemy whispered, barely audible. "SAY SOMETHING?" This time she yelled loud enough that Madeline was sure Leo heard her in the hospital thirty miles away.

"What is there to say, Madeline? For the past months, you have been lying to us. Even worse, you lied to ME no more than 3 hours ago! What do you want to hear? What am I *possibly* supposed to say to you? You tried to take my grandfather's home right out from under his feet! And, yes, I DO think you are a terrible person!"

"I know, I know! But when I got here, and I met Leo, and I met you...and when I saw the house...I don't know. I couldn't do it. I never even tried to bring up the subject with Leo. And now all I want to do is to help. I don't want them tearing down your grandfather's home and building a road through it!" Tears surfaced in Madeline's eyes, but she held them back. Even though she was trying to be strong, Alchemy could see right through to Madeline's anguish.

Alchemy was mad, there was no doubt about that, and at the same time, she had known something was up all along. Should she have been expecting this? And looking at Madeline just then, it was hard to stay mad at her. The tears by now were no longer strangled at the source but instead flowing freely down her face. Anyone could cry on demand, Alchemy realized, but there was something genuine in Madeline's face that Alchemy couldn't ignore.

"I really do want to help," Madeline sniffled between gasps for air.

"I know you do," Alchemy surprised herself at how calm she was being about this. Normally, she would have just started right in on Madeline, but if Madeline really wanted to help now, Alchemy figured they could use all the help they could get to try to save Leo's house.

"What's in your hand, Maddy?" Alchemy only just now realized that Madeline had been holding something the entire time.

"This?" Madeline looked at the note, "This may be one of the ways that we can save the house."

Madeline held out the note and ring to Alchemy. After Alchemy finished reading it, she looked up.

"Isn't your last name Hightower?" Alchemy asked Madeline.

"Yes, it is," Madeline reached for the picture to show Alchemy. "Look how happy Adeline looks with him."

"Madeline!" Alchemy shouted, "You and this Adeline woman look exactly the same, and you both have the same last names! You must be related to her! And I know how we can find out. Follow me!"

Alchemy grabbed Madeline by the hand and led her down the hall to the office in the back of the house. She walked in and immediately began searching for something, but Madeline wasn't sure what, so she just stood there watching. A couple minutes later, Alchemy emerged from inside the closet with a large book.

"This book has every person who has ever lived here in it, along with the families, traced back as far as it could go, a brief description about them, and other family-related things. I've seen it once before, but I put it back and never got around to looking at it again."

"Where did it come from?" asked Madeline.

"The people who my grandfather's family bought the house from made it, kind of like a tribute to the house or something I guess. All I know is that it took them years to finish."

"What was the date on that picture?" Alchemy demanded.

"September 16, 1864," Madeline said.

"1864, 1864..." Alchemy was repeating the year aloud as she flipped through the pages.

"Here it is!"

During and following the years after the Civil War, Cedarvine Manor was used as a convalescent infirmary for the Union and Confederate soldiers injured in bat-

tle. Doctor Phillip Newborne Jennings who was in charge of the operation was assisted by his team of nurses, including his cousin Adeline Hightower.

"This is so exciting!" Alchemy squealed.

She handed the book over to Madeline. On the opposite page was the family tree of Dr. Jennings and Adeline Hightower. Madeline noticed that Adeline had no children or had ever married anyone, but Adeline's brother Johnathan Hightower did. He was the only other one with that last name. Madeline kept reading trying to find a name that was familiar to her. It ended with Benjamin Hightower and Patricia Dorris. They were her grandparents!

"I can't believe it," whispered Madeline in complete shock. Alchemy, curious as to what was not believable, leaned forward to get a better look.

"What is it?" Alchemy asked, "What can't you believe?"

"Right here," Madeline shoved the book into Alchemy's hands. "These two people here, where this family tree ends, they are my grandparents. That means this guy Jonathan Hightower is my great-great-great grandfather. Jonathan and Adeline were brother and sister, so that makes her my great-great-great aunt."

"Wow! Madeline, that is so cool! You are related to like the very first owners of this house! Maybe it wasn't a coincidence that you came here or even a bad thing. Maybe this was supposed to happen. How could you let this house be torn down when it's just as much a part of your history as it is Grandpa's or mine?"

"Alchemy, I had NO idea I was in any way related to this family, and my mother and father were always tight-lipped about our relations, and..."

Madeline was deep in thought yet again. All the pieces to the puzzle were falling into place now. The ring, the pictures, the book, Adeline, Jacob Mordecai Lee, the infirmary, Dr. Jennings...this house was full of important history. How could she use it to help save the house? She thought of her father, and then she thought of the man who seemed more like a father to her...Leo. She thought about him just lying there in that cold, sterile hospital bed.

"Alchemy, in all the excitement, I forgot to ask. How is Leo doing?" Madeline questioned.

"Well, I talked to my dad. He had trouble getting back when Leo first went to the hospital. He's always at the whim of government scheduling since his job involves inspecting military bases. He is wait-listed like all other military personnel. He should arrive late this afternoon, and he is going to pick up

Grandpa and bring him back tonight in time for dinner." Alchemy paused and looked at Madeline, "You're going to tell him, right?"

Madeline swallowed, almost too ashamed to even answer. "I've not met your father. It's going to be hard enough telling Leo, but admitting my guilt to a complete stranger is probably exactly what I deserve. Of course, I'm going to tell them. I have to tell them, even though it isn't going to be easy. Will your aunt and uncle be here, too?"

"They may stop by after church tonight, especially with Grandpa Leo coming home, but if we're lucky, they won't," Alchemy hopefully added. "My dad is a great guy. He's not going to be happy, but he loves this house like we do, and I know when the dust clears, he'll jump right in with both feet to save the place."

Madeline closed her eyes and took a deep breath for the ordeal she knew she would soon face. She was ready...very ready.

CHAPTER 17

Cedarvine Manor, May 2003

"Alchemy, I don't think I can do this," Madeline said as she paced the room. John, Alchemy's father, would be here with Leo any minute, and Madeline was beginning to get nervous.

Alchemy grabbed her arm, and Maddy stopped pacing as she looked in Alchemy's eyes. "Hey, it'll be okay. Grandpa is tough. He can handle it. Besides, it wouldn't be right to keep lying to him. That would be worse than telling him the truth."

"I know, I know. I'm just dreading the look on his face when I tell him. I just know it's going to break his heart."

There was a silence and then they both looked to the door as they heard a car door slam shut. Madeline grabbed Alchemy's hand and squeezed it. Leo came through the front door, leaning on a man's arm. Madeline couldn't see the man's face very clearly, but she did catch a glimpse of his green eyes before he bent his head to say something to Leo. She let go of Alchemy's hand and straightened up and lifted her chin. "Leo, it's nice to have you back home."

Alchemy squealed and ran to hug the two favorite men in her life. Leo looked up and smiled, and at the same time, John looked up. As soon as their eyes met, Maddy felt something like an electric shock. He was tall and muscular, with a dark brown crew cut. She tore her eyes away from his face, which was very hard to do because he had the most captivating face. She cleared her throat, feeling her resolve withering away, the doubt returning.

John extended his hand, looked directly back at her and said, "Leo's been telling me all about you, Madeline."

Unsure of his meaning, Madeline floundered for something to say.

Alchemy interrupted, "Grandpa, Madeline has something she wants to tell you," as she pushed Madeline forward meaningfully and then whispered, "You might as well get it over with."

"Okay, okay." She spoke to Leo and John, saying, "You two had better come over here and sit down."

"Is there something wrong?" Leo asked as he and John made their way into the middle of the foyer.

"You have no idea," Madeline muttered to herself.

"Well, if we're about to receive bad news, we might as well have it in the kitchen with a nice cup of coffee and maybe a piece of that cake you promised me when you last came to visit me in the hospital," said Leo.

Going into the kitchen, Alchemy whispered, "Stop trying to delay it. Just blurt it all out."

Madeline replied, "I'm not delaying anything." John hadn't said anything further, but his gaze had never left Madeline.

After everyone was seated with cake and coffee in front them, Madeline cleared her throat once again, and after being kicked under the table in the shin by Alchemy, she blurted the whole thing out. Madeline didn't look up to see the expression on Leo's face, and she was pretty sure John's face wouldn't betray anything, which was worse than knowing.

"Leo, I'm not a nurse. I work at TREC. They sent me here to try to persuade you to sell. I'm sorry. When I came here I was mentally drained. I didn't think that I would be able to feel anything towards another human being ever again, after Ron…" Madeline's voice broke. "That doesn't matter now. What matters is that I betrayed the only person who has ever shown me any compassion. The person who became like the father I've never had. I *will* understand if you don't forgive me."

She held up her head and met Leo's steady gaze. His face was impassive.

"You must allow me to help you protect this house. The more I have seen of it, the more convinced I've become that it can be saved based on its historical background. Before you got home, Alchemy and I discussed all of the possibilities, and we both agree that we have enough historical proof to put up a good fight."

She stopped and Alchemy came to her rescue saying, "If you don't forgive her, then you are both heartless. She is the only one who can save this house. Give her a chance to redeem herself."

"Alchemy, I have every intention of forgiving Maddy," Leo said as he gave Madeline an affectionate look. Madeline was speechless. She had fully expected to be tossed out on her head. Everyone looked over at John, who hadn't said a word. Madeline swallowed wondering what he would say. He looked so impenetrable.

"What kind of historical proof did you come up with?" John icily inquired, but the ice wasn't in his eyes. Alchemy, who had been fidgeting while she waited for her father to say something, saw the compassion in his eyes. She was worried at what he might say, but now she jumped up with a cry of glee and hugged her father fiercely. He smiled at her and patted her on the head. Then they all looked at Madeline expectantly.

"Well, we'll start with the little things in the house, like the leather book, the documents, the list and pictures of patients who were treated here. Also, we'll catalogue the journals, the pictures, and we'll call the Center for Historic Preservation at Middle Tennessee State University. Certainly, the writing on the wall will find favor with the folks at the Historical Registry. Another huge factor, I think, is going to be the house and the surrounding land. There is a Tennessee cemetery law of preservation, and the old gravestones over behind the old stables should help us out tremendously. Oh, there are so many things to do, and I want to get started, now!"

Leo, John, and Alchemy stared at Madeline, but smiles broke out all around when she suddenly stopped and saw the expressions on their faces. That huge dam of shame locked around her heart broke open, and the healing waters of finally telling the truth soaked through Madeline. Or maybe it was the tears she had let freely flow. All she knew was that she was ready to fight.

CHAPTER 18

Cedarvine Manor, May 2003

How could I have ever even liked him, let alone wanted to marry him? She pondered that when she saw that snake of a man slither up the walk. Ron had told her that he had some concerns that he wished to discuss, and Madeline was more than ready to discuss them. *I fell for his stories like some helpless teen every time! Not this time.* The vow was cement hard. The *big* shock that she had for Ron floated to the surface, causing a grin to erupt on her face.

Alchemy was outside when Ron drove up. He barely glanced her way, but the small glance he gave her was filled with disgust. "You got a problem, mister?" Alchemy growled.

Ron turned away from her dismissively and said, "Madeline, *sweet girl*," as he stepped out of his silver Lexus with the plush leather seats. He obviously took her grin to be something completely different than what it truly was.

"Keep it strictly business, if you can. Now, what was it that you wanted to talk to me about so urgently?" Madeline was curious because he never made appearances unless it was imperative to *his* career or *his* wellbeing. When they had been planning their wedding, he had even scheduled the ceremony late enough so that he could go to work that day and *then* get married!

"Come now, *my dear*. I have news that you might want to hear!" He thought that he could dangle his smooth-talking ways in front of Madeline and that she would take the bait.

"Stop with the names, and just tell me why you're here! Last I checked, I no longer work for you." Madeline paused to take in his surprised expression. "Yes, my resignation is here in my hand and will be officially on your desk in the morning. Also, my father will know, too, in case you were wondering," she calmly replied to the look of utter disbelief on Ron's sculpted face.

"You what?! There is no way that you would do something so, so...rash!" he stammered. Madeline was getting irritated just looking at him and wished that he would just come out with it, so she asked, "Now, what is this news that you drove all the way out here to tell me?"

"Oh, yes, the big news!" Ron continued on flawlessly, "We, or should I say *I*, have managed to pull some strings; the old coot will have to sell the house now. I've had the planning commission board condemn the home and land so he will have to sell!"

Madeline couldn't believe the audacity of Ron. He had no qualms about kicking Leo out of his home, just so he would get a bigger office and a substantial raise to boot!

"Ron, *honey*," Madeline cooed as loving as one could manage to such a vile human being, "if you even think that you are going to get away with this while I'm alive, you have one enormous ego and a head of air to match! This is one time that I'll refuse to turn the other cheek." Madeline turned to walk back into the house, but Ron had another idea. He followed her up the path to the heavy front doors.

"I **WILL** build this road through here if that means burying everyone here under the tar, and that includes you, *my dear!*"

Madeline spun on her heels, finding herself standing nose to nose with him. "If you ever bother Leo Dunn or anyone else who has the most remote connection with this house or property ever again, I will come after you!" Flames erupted from her icy-blue eyes. "Not only that, but I will track you down and ensure that you pay!"

"Are you threatening me, *Miss Hightower*? Because if you are, *I* will make *your* life a living hell!"

That was it! If she didn't walk back into the house now, she was going to stoop to his level, and that level would be a disgrace.

"Ron, leave now," she warned from the doorway in a calm voice that could have frozen a flame. Ron made a move to enter, causing her to act the only way she knew how.

She heard the '*CRACK*' as the door made contact with his nose, and at the same time, she heard a gleeful squeal out of Alchemy who had observed the entire exchange. In one fell swoop, she had closed the door on her past, literally. At one time, knowing the end of a relationship had occurred would have broken her heart. Now the sound of him wailing in pain and anger was music to her ears; she almost reveled in the noise. She heard Alchemy unceremoniously direct him back to the road, heard his car tires spin on the gravel of the round-a-bout in the side courtyard, and then she smiled as Alchemy entered the manor. The moment Alchemy entered the house, Madeline felt a new buoyancy. Alchemy smiled mischievously at Madeline as she headed to the kitchen for her daily Coke.

Madeline decided that she needed to go and make sure that Leo was all right. The fight had not disturbed his rest, thankfully. When she returned to the hall, she noticed John looking intently at her from the second story staircase landing. Once again, that electric shock rang through Madeline. She couldn't help but shiver a bit as he returned the look.

"Oh, hi! I didn't see you there," she started. His inquisitive look prompted her to explain herself. "That was my ex-fiancé. He said he had something to tell me, but I think I had more to tell him…and if it disturbed you…I'm very sorry," Madeline stammered, not sure what else to say.

He simply nodded his head. The simple movement impelled Madeline to be bold. "Would you like to go for a walk? Perhaps I could explain better…" she implored.

"I would love to take a walk," he replied as he walked slowly down the steps toward Madeline.

They left the house, using the side door facing the old abandoned chicken coop in complete silence. Not a word was spoken between the two. Madeline didn't consider it an awkward silence; it was in some surreal way…pleasant? It was quite odd but reassuring to her.

After walking a short distance from the house Madeline blurted out, "I never wanted to push anyone out…"

"It's okay. I understand," he interrupted her. She didn't care if he thought that it was *okay,* she was still going to explain.

"I only accepted this job out of anger toward my father, who just happens to be my boss, and his little stooge, my ex, who was here this morning. But when I arrived, I fell under the spell of your dad and this house. I never wanted to hurt anyone. I'm telling the truth, and I honestly want to help you all to save this magical home. It's part of *me*, too. I've always wanted to know my history, the stories of my relatives, and my father just wouldn't talk about it. He forbade my mother, too…why did she listen to him?" Madeline took a deep, calming breath after pouring her heart out.

John took her elbow and led her toward the old stable. "I've come to realize that much. I mean, from Alchemy and Dad have told me, I can tell that you care almost as much as Alchemy and I do about Dad and this manor. Maybe in time, we'll be able to bring my brother and sister around to our way of thinking. Now, even as much as I don't want to admit it, I'm really glad to have you here, Madeline."

"Maddy," she corrected.

"Maddy?" He tested it out, "I like that much better than Madeline."

He smiled. *Another electric shock…!*

They spent several pleasurable hours walking the property as they discussed their pasts and what they wanted in their futures. He revealed that he wanted to leave the service to settle down and give Alchemy a stable home. He was tired of traveling from place to place inspecting bases for the U.S. government, especially overseas. Another wish that he had was to live near this house and his beloved father. Madeline told him of her early years, her own "broken" home and how she wished to flee as far from her father as humanly possible. She opened up her heart in a way she hadn't thought possible ever again. Embarrassed by baring her soul, talk finally turned to John and his past. It was going to have to wait for another day, as he suggested that they go back to the house to check on Leo.

On that note, they began to walk back to the house. Madeline slowed her pace, reluctant for this walk to end. *Was it over so soon? She really didn't want it to end so soon, but…*

There was a house to save.

CHAPTER 19

TREC Headquarters, Nashville, May 2003

"Good morning, Madeline," Jennings Hightower sternly greeted his daughter as she entered the inner sanctum of his office. "I'd ask what I owe this early morning visit of yours to, but Ron already apprised me of your foolish plans."

"Father, I would hardly call it foolish to preserve what little piece of family I still have left, a family I knew nothing about!"

Jennings' startled look encouraged Madeline. "That's right, *my* family, *our* family! How could you even think of destroying it, Father?"

"Madeline, whatever are you talking about? Ron was right…you're suffering from some sort of delusion. He said you were acting strangely. Said you were in cahoots with some cult girl and her father. Said they must have brainwashed you. Said you viciously attacked him! Whatever has gotten into you, Madeline? Your mother and I didn't raise you to…"

"Don't you dare bring mother into this! You didn't raise me. I raised myself. You were never there when Mother was sick, you never were there for anything I did in school, and the only time you were THERE for me, you ruined my life, and…"

Oh, Madeline, there you go with your histrionics once again. I would hardly call *saving* you from a mediocre life with a farmer ruination! We planned a much higher station in life for you, and we gave you everything you needed to take your rightful place in society. I've groomed Ron to take my place, and he has all the attributes necessary for a successful life. How can you throw all that away! What is it with you, Madeline? Why do you try to destroy all the good things I've done for you??"

Madeline stood rooted in front of her father, and for once, she wasn't going to back down. "Destroy is a word that you thrive on, Father. I've never once *not* done what you asked, even when my heart was breaking. All my life I've played the dutiful daughter. When mother was ill, where were you? I never left her side. I went to school like all the other kids, but I never had the chance to make real friends, or climb a tree, or just act like a normal kid! You could have tried to give me a normal childhood, but even then, you were driven to destroy anything which got in the way of building a road. Just like you tore down trees or buildings, or rock walls, you tore my childhood away from me. I didn't know kids were supposed to run and play and fall down and get back up. I didn't even know what being in a family felt like until I met Mike, and then you destroyed that, too. I've given you my devotion as a child and as an adult, but I can't sit by one more day and let you destroy something that's more valuable than any road."

Jennings' normally stoic, unruffled demeanor seemed to slip a notch at Madeline's tirade, but he quickly recovered by saying, "Madeline, how dare you speak to me in such a manner and tone! That family at Cedarvine must be everything Ron says they are…uncultured hicks, with a strange hold over you."

"Oh, Father, just once would you listen to me? I'm not a young girl anymore who you can spirit away to let *someone else* have a hold over me. Mrs. DuBois couldn't take mother's place, not that you even thought about that. Social graces? Who cares? I certainly didn't. I don't want to fit into the mold you've made for me. You just wanted me away from Mike, from a life on a *farm* that you considered beneath me. Well, guess what, father? I'm going to be on a *farm*, a beautiful *farm*, and a *farm* that is part of our family!"

At the look of shock on Jennings's face, Madeline knew she had discovered something that would finally shake the tightly held reins of control her father exerted. "That's right. Cedarvine Manor is part of our history, Father. A lovely story, Father, about doctors and nurses and soldiers and writing on the wall."

"Madeline, I'm not interested in fairy tales. I have a business to run, and you have a job to do, and I've heard enough nonsense from you on this subject!"

"Oh, no, Father, I've just begun. And you'll listen to me. Your great-great grandfather was *Johnathan* Hightower, and his sister Adeline nursed with her cousin Dr. Phillip Newborne Jennings. Your parents must have named you after Dr. Jennings. I look exactly like Adeline, Father! She's a part of me, of my family. Why wouldn't you want me to know my family??"

"*That* family? The romanticized version of *that* family? Oh, Madeline, a country doctor and an old-maid aunt? You find *that* appealing family history? *That* once-fine manor turned into a working farm during Reconstruction, and *that* working farm killed my father and mother. Oh, not literally, but after they were forced to sell Cedarvine, my mother, and especially my father, were never the same. When I was born near the end of the depression, my parents were still trying to recover from what they went through on that farm. My father just couldn't get beyond it. My mother loved that house but hated what it did to my father. It made me glad to know it passed into someone else's hands. The Dunn's haven't been able to do much more with it either, but I will not allow my daughter to be part of *that* farm!!"

Madeline shook her head in disbelief. No wonder her father had been so adamant about this project, but she still refused to let his "'history" destroy one more thing in her life. She needed this history, this family, this farm.

"Father, I'm so sorry for the pain you must have suffered, but your anger is misplaced. Your anger kept this very special place out of my life, and I'm not a little girl anymore who you can order around. If you try to fight me on this, I'll pull out every historical preservationist in this country and hound you until you give up the fight."

"Do you think a few tree-hugging preservations and a disloyal daughter can keep me from tearing down that eyesore? Have you thought of the jobs you'll be taking from people, Madeline? Have you thought about the money to be made from this project? Have you thought of the glory this could bring to the firm? Have you thought about…"

"Father, enough. You'll find other roads to build, other jobs to line your pockets, more *glory* for the company, but you'll not find it in the boundaries of Cedarvine. I'll fight you on this with every ounce of my being, Father, don't think I won't."

With a rising awareness, Jennings saw that his daughter truly meant to defy him. "You have no idea what you're getting into, Madeline. I can't believe you would go against your upbringing, your inheritance here at the firm, against me?!"

"I know exactly what I'm getting into, Father, and I will fight for it with all of my being. I don't want a single thing from you. I think you've given me quite enough."

As she turned to walk out the door, she looked over her shoulder and straight into her father's eyes. "I wouldn't fight this, Father. I would think by now that you really should have seen *the writing on the wall.*"

CHAPTER 20

Cedarvine Manor, July 2003

Alchemy shifted in the black leather chair, her black hair falling in her face. Grumbling, she shoved it out of the way. What in the world were they going to do? They had to think of something. So many things had been thrown into the air—a historic society, a museum, a house on the national tour registry—but nothing seemed to hit a mark. She looked around the house. What in the world could they do with the house to save it, to earn enough money to keep it going? They had to come up with something to keep Aunt Melissa and Uncle David off their backs, too, about selling Cedarvine, what they had come to call Leo's White Elephant. Maybe something with events and people, though those were two things she really didn't like. Maybe, just maybe…it could be a good business.

"A bed and breakfast," Alchemy voiced without her really knowing it. She shook her head, and then smiled when she realized she had caught the attention of her father, Madeline, and Grandpa Leo.

"What was that?" her grandfather questioned leaning forward out of his chair on his cane.

"A bed and breakfast would work," Alchemy said again looking at them.

"That's a tremendous idea, Alchemy," Maddy agreed looking at her with a smile, the red flames of her hair falling around her face as her blue eyes sparkled.

"That is a good idea," John chimed in. Only Leo had seemed put off by the idea at the time, but they had been having these discussions for weeks now on what to do with the manor. Leo wasn't quite convinced. It wasn't until the letter they'd been waiting for from the National Registry arrived, that Leo realized that to save his home, it needed to be protected. A bed and breakfast was the most foolproof and financially feasible option. He could still live there, share his knowledge and love of the manor, and make new friends. He threw his proverbial hat into the ring and joyously joined the three people who meant so much to him.

🍁   🍁   🍁

Eight months later, Maddy shifted in her seat, and looked over at Alchemy who was leaning over a book filled with strips of different paint samples. They were finalizing the last few colors needed for the last of the renovated rooms. The majority of the rooms were painted and wall-papered, except one, of course. Special care had been taken with the room where the writing had become the centerpiece of the preservation fight, which they had won. The dingy yellow room was going to be painted a newer brighter color, and the room that had been Alchemy's was going to be painted a rose color. Leo's old room was going to be painted a dark scarlet. Seeing a color she liked, Maddy set it aside with the lilac color with which they were going to paint her now-vacated room.

"How about this color?" Alchemy said leaning over and pointing out a white paint she liked. Maddy wasn't sure what the difference was, considering there seemed to be a million shades of white.

"What room would it go in?" Maddy questioned, looking at the blueprint of the upstairs.

"This one," Alchemy said pointing to the room to the right of the office door.

Yes, the room to the right of the office door, the room named after her father…the Jennings' Suite. In the eight months since their hurtful words, Madeline had found a new peace, especially since the day four months ago when she had answered the ringing of the doorbell. There stood her father.

He seemed awkward, uncomfortable, and ready to walk off and abandon his purpose. Madeline asked him what he wanted.

"Madeline," he said, "I apologize."

Those were words she never thought she'd hear him say.

"You're a grown woman. You can make your own decisions without me, and I'm sorry for my faults as your father."

She tried to shake her head, taken aback by his fumbled words. He had never seemed old to her, but he did at that moment.

"No," he continued, "I was never a perfect father. I know that. I wanted so much for you to succeed, so you could be happy. But without your mother, I felt so lost, and I wasn't quite sure what to do with you."

"But I am happy, Father. Maybe not in the way you wanted, but I am."

He smiled at her. "Then that is all that matters."

She invited him inside.

"Well, Father, what do you think?"

The look of wonder on Jennings' face mirrored the sparkling chandelier overhead, the one Madeline had painstakingly cleaned and restored. Madeline gave him time to come to grips with whatever he was feeling.

"The piano's still there…just as my mother described," Jennings whispered.

Madeline knew the power of this beautiful centerpiece of the house, and she hoped her father sensed it, too.

"I never lived here, Madeline. My parents sold Cedarvine to the Dunn's long before I was born. I just remember my father's stories of the hardships they suffered attempting to farm. My father turned into a bitter old man, and all I remember growing up is hearing my father's awful curses about Cedarvine being the cause of his misery. They never recovered financially from the loss of Cedarvine, and then the Depression added to their poverty. I grew up being made fun of for my 'country' clothes, and I vowed when I could be on my own that I would NEVER be poor again."

Madeline looked in wonder at her father. He must have had a horrible childhood. She felt the stirrings of forgiveness in her heart.

After their confrontation, she had worried that she might never see her father again. Despite all that had happened, he was still her father, and she couldn't stop loving him. It never occurred to her that he might feel the same.

"I…I…can't believe I'm standing here, Madeline," Jennings said as he cleared his throat.

"I'm glad you're standing here, too. I have so much to share with you. Will you let me?"

He had nodded solemnly.

Since that day, she'd seen more of her father. They would have lunch together or just sit and talk. She would mostly talk about the Manor, and he would listen. She was sure he cancelled business engagements to be with her, though he never came out and admitted it.

He became a rather constant guest. Leo came to enjoy the talks they had about Cedarvine's history, John gladly accepted Jennings' engineering advice, and Alchemy thrilled in having another grandfather figure, who also spoiled her. She especially felt a deep and abiding love for Madeline who had brought Alchemy the mother figure she had so missed.

When they decided to name the suites in the Manor for the bed and breakfast brochure, no one was more surprised than Jennings when they presented him with the plaque which would be mounted outside the room.

"I don't know what to say. I'm speechless…"

"Father, you've been such a tremendous help to us. You've given us advice, money, called in favors from your business contacts to help complete this project, and Cedarvine truly is a part of your heritage. You're in good company with Adeline and Mordecai."

"You've given me far more than I deserve, Madeline. All of you have. After what I tried to do…"

Leo jumped in with, "What's past is past, Jennings. Let it go. We have a wonderful future to look forward to, and we're glad you're a part of it."

Alchemy and John added resounding agreement, and they all went upstairs to the bedroom to the right of the office. Jennings slid the plaque into the mounted holder on the wall. He looked across to the room where it had all begun. He silently thanked all the souls before him for finally making him see the 'writing on the wall.'

Coming out of her reveries, Maddy said, "That color sounds good, Alchemy. My father would approve." She went back to looking at the colors while Alchemy circled the color of white she had chosen and set it in the pile with the other colors. They had just decided on two more colors, when John walked into the house.

"Hello," John greeted kissing both her and Alchemy on the cheeks. "So have you two finished choosing the colors yet?"

"Yes, we just finished. How is it going out there?" Alchemy asked looking up at her dad, then at Maddy.

"Good. We're almost finished with the center, and the amphitheatre was finished yesterday. All that really needs to be finished is the painting of the final rooms in the house, the pond needs to be filled, and the courtyard needs to be cleaned out so the brickwork can be done," her father continued after he had taken a drink of Alchemy's coke that was sitting on the table. "Do you want to come see it?"

"Sure, why not," Maddy said standing up. Alchemy nodded her head in agreement, and she followed Maddy and her dad out of the house over to the soon-to-be-finished courtyard. Right now it was just a place where they were tossing trash and unnecessary supplies. They continued on to what had once been the mule stables, now miraculously transformed with the help of Jennings' expertise, into a lovely dining area with warm knotty pine walls and floors. John held the door open for Maddy and Alchemy and then followed them inside the now-finished center. A few of the workers were putting the finishing touches on the lights, while the rest of them finished setting up the tables and chairs that designated the dining area.

After her dad finished talking to a few of the men who were working, he showed them the amphitheatre that had been completed the day before but still had a rustic, old-time feel to it. He showed them the now-clean pavilion that they had turned into a barbecue house and the limestone parking area. As they walked past the pond, she saw that it only needed water and the fish and the turtles that they had talked about. The rustic cabin had been finished earlier in the week. All that needed to be completed were the few remaining rooms in the manor and the courtyard leading to it.

Holding hands, John and Maddy walked toward the house. Alchemy smiled.

Epilogue

❀

Cedarvine Manor Bed and Breakfast, June 2004

The crowd gathered outdoors for the ceremony. A small area furnished with white chairs created a warm focus on a beautiful wooden gazebo. The gazebo was decorated in pink and white flowers and matching streamers. A small band played off to the right, consisting of a cello, a violin, and a flute player. All the people were dressed in their finest summer wardrobe. The ladies had brightly-colored sundresses on with big floppy hats to match, while the men wore light-colored dress slacks and lightweight button-up shirts. The guests took their seats and grew quiet. The band started playing again, and all heads turned to the back of the lovely outdoor area.

Madeline appeared, a vision in white, her beautiful curls pinned up on top of her head and her blue eyes sparkling. All attention was on her now. Leo and her father walked up beside her, and as Leo winked at her, Jennings placed his arm in hers and began to accompany her down the aisle. They stopped a few feet away from the gazebo. Jennings bent down and kissed her on the cheek.

"Thank you so much for making me understand," Jennings whispered to his daughter. "You helped me accept my past. I love you."

Madeline wasn't sure, but she thought she might have seen a tear in his eye before he turned and walked away. She was overjoyed that they had both been able to be a part of saving Cedarvine, and at the same time, she was happy at saving her relationship with her father. All of her life, Jennings had seemed a cold person with no heart, but after the whole fiasco with Ron, the deception they had created, and the subsequent refurbishing of the Manor, he had taken on an all-new personality. When he retired and sold the firm, (something that Madeline thought would never happen) he had grudgingly, though only at first, advised John on the best and most economically feasible way to connect roads throughout the complex. As he came to spend more time at Cedarvine, he knew he had been wrong to keep Madeline from it. His new-found energy exerted itself in helping his daughter and her "new" family at Cedarvine, and he even had recently enrolled in a swing dancing class where he was becoming quite friendly with his new dance partner.

Madeline's attention was drawn back to the gazebo and her big day.

She continued up the steps of the gazebo and stood face to face with the man who she knew was the love of her life…John. She had all the people she cared for the most around her. Her father, Leo as John's best man, Alchemy as her maid of honor, and they were at the place that they all cared about the most: Cedarvine.

The past year had been a crazy one but a good one at that. Madeline, Leo, and John had been extremely busy trying to save Cedarvine Manor from destruction, and after that goal was accomplished, they had to figure out what to do with the old house. Alchemy's ideas on turning the house into a bed and breakfast seemed the clear winner. The house had lots of rooms, it was in a great location, and John, Madeline, Alchemy, and Leo could still live there and manage it.

So much work had to be done, and they thought that they would never be finished. Even David and Melissa had given up their doubts and fears for Leo when they saw how much more alive he seemed in the planning and executing of the bed and breakfast project over the last year. Cedarvine Manor was well overdue for a facelift. After that, all new furniture was bought to replace the old, destroyed pieces. They cleaned up the pond, perfected the landscape, renovated the barns and sheds, and bought some horses and ducks. It seemed that everyone was too busy to even breathe, but John and Madeline hadn't been too busy for each other.

In the months leading up to the grand opening of Cedarvine Manor, John and Madeline worked together on the house. In that time they formed a loving relationship that grew with the normal things: going on dates, walking around the house and grounds, engaging in frequent conversations, and becoming daily more in tune with one another. Before she knew it, John popped the question and Madeline accepted. They broke the news to everyone else the next day.

Luckily for them, Cedarvine Manor was nearly complete, and the first big event to be held there was going to be John and Madeline's wedding on this beautiful June day. The ceremony completed Madeline's happiness, and afterwards, the music played in the banquet hall where the reception was being held. The guests enjoyed themselves, wonderful food was served, and everyone danced long into the evening.

"Hello, Mr. and Mrs. Dunn," Leo winked at the newly married couple. "How does it feel to be married?" As he pulled Madeline's hand to his lips, the sparkle of what they had come to call "Addie's Ring" threw brilliant facets of light his way.

"It feels wonderful!" Madeline exclaimed and leaned in to give John a small kiss on the cheek.

"Yes, it certainly does," John said, never taking his eyes off of Madeline as he, too, kissed the top of her head, while gently rubbing the ring on her finger.

"Well, you two go on and talk to your guests; meanwhile, I'm going to find my girl Alchemy and ask for a dance." Leo headed off in the other direction.

Madeline and John continued smiling at one another.

"I never actually thought this would happen," Madeline told John, "I mean, that I would ever get married."

"And I never thought that I would find someone like you." John leaned in for another kiss.

🍁   🍁   🍁

Inside the house, all was quiet. The music could be faintly heard from the reception area. In the room at the end of the hall, standing in front of the window surveying the party below, was the ghostly silhouette of a woman in a nurse's outfit, with curly hair pulled up under her cap. She stood there for a long moment staring out the window, when a hand reached out from behind her and rested on her shoulder. Startled, the woman turned around, face to face with a handsome, clean-cut man in a soldier's uniform.

"I thought you would never find me," whispered Adeline as she stretched her arms around the man and held him in a tight embrace.

"And now that I have, I'll never let you go again, my beautiful dreamer," whispered Mordy as he kissed the top of the woman's head. The two drifted gracefully toward the newly whitewashed and restored wall which held the story of so many, certain that the writing on the wall would continue to give peace to those who viewed its wonder.

About the Author

Dina Bozsoki and the Wilson Central Scribes wrote this novel as part of a creative writing class at Wilson Central High School. Dina Bozsoki has taught English, mostly composition, for 32 years in Illinois and Tennessee. She also advises the award-winning *Blue Prints* yearbook.

978-0-595-39269-8
0-595-39269-5

Printed in the United States
50447LVS00004B/28-204

9 780595 392698